Through Each Other's Eyes

By:

Aleena Ashe

ISBN: 9781797799056

Chapter 1: Elizabeth

Elizabeth couldn't take it anymore. Tonight was supposed to be perfect. She would dance with Wickham, Jane would dance with Bingley, perhaps he would even propose. But no, her family chose to seize every possible opportunity to look ridiculous! Mr. Collins had stepped on her toes several times almost ruining her slippers, her mother was crass, her two youngest sisters had clearly been drinking and flirted openly with every officer they saw, Mary exhibited her 'talent' on the pianoforte for far too long, and *then,* as if that were not enough, her father chose to remove Mary in such a way that it was obvious to all the world that she was humiliated.

Only she and Jane had behaved themselves and if she were honest, Elizabeth had to admit that she had been rude out of spite to both Miss Bingley and Mr. Darcy. But who could blame her? Caroline Bingley was pretentious and haughty coming over to give her advice about Wickham. As if she had any right! And Mr. Darcy! What was he about? He asked her to dance, then he had barely spoken - as usual. When he did speak, it was as if he was pained to do so. However, his anger at the mention of Wickham proved that she had hit the mark! He clearly did not like being reminded of his misdeeds in that arena.

Needing air, Elizabeth stepped out onto the balcony and sipping her glass of punch stared up at the night sky. The cool air was refreshing and she felt her temper ebb slightly. Without realizing it her thoughts took her back to her dance with Mr. Darcy. He truly was an excellent dancer. He must have had the finest tutors. In fact, she couldn't truly think of any *faults* in his manners, other than at the assembly. Since then, he had not been as amiable as Mr. Bingley but he was not officious beyond what one might expect from his set. However, she couldn't seem to accurately sketch his character. She heard so many varying accounts. Wickham had told her his tale of woe and she had seen how they acted toward each other that day in Meryton. Would Mr. Bingley choose to befriend a man who could be so cruel as Lt. Wickham had said? The fact that Mr. Bingley's fortune was from trade didn't seem to bother Mr. Darcy at all. What did that say about the man? Perhaps he was less stodgy than she thought. Charlotte seemed to think he was perhaps just uncomfortable around new people; that he in fact, liked Elizabeth very much and was unsure how to act around her.

Looking up at the numerous stars always brought Elizabeth peace. They reminded her how small she was and how her problems meant nothing in the grand scheme of things. When she saw a shooting star she closed her eyes and made her wish: "I wish, just once, I could understand why some people (thinking of Mr. Darcy) act the way they do." Opening her eyes, she took a deep breath, smoothed her hair to undo any damage caused by the breeze, and returned to the ballroom.

*****

Darcy

Darcy just needed to escape the ball for 5 minutes. Then he could trust himself to return and be civil to Bingley's guests. 'Why? Why do I have this ridiculous need to gain her approval? Miss Elizabeth Bennet is not for me. Yes, she may be beautiful - not in the classical sense but in an intelligent, beguiling way that I cannot ignore - but her family! Egad, they're atrocious. Never in my life have I witnessed so many breaches of propriety go unchecked. The mother, the sisters, even tonight her father had behaved in a way I cannot not countenance. As if that were not enough, her smarmy cousin waltzed right up to me and began speaking some nonsense about my Aunt Catherine as if we were old friends. We have not even been introduced! Can you imagine?'

'Despite all that, I want her. I want to know her innermost thoughts, I want to hear her laugh, see her smile, walk with her in the gardens at Pemberley, hold her in my arms and… enough of that. I will not be fit for company if I allow my thoughts to travel *that* road.'

'Despite my efforts to get to know her by listening to her conversations, our little friendly debates, I feel as though I am no closer to understanding her than when we met. It is as if she rebels against my every attempt to get close to her. I am utterly confounded. Never has a woman even disagreed with me, much less thrown barbs at me as she did tonight. I can only hope Wickham has not gotten his hooks into her. Even if she dislikes me, I could not rest knowing he may do her harm.'

Staring blankly out the window, he noticed a flash of light. 'Ah, a shooting star.' Without really thinking about it, he made a wish. "I wish I knew what makes Miss Elizabeth tick."

Hearing the door open behind him, he turned. "Ah, there you are Darcy! Come back out to the ball. I'll not have you hiding away while I play host!" With a sigh, he rejoined the mass of people crowding the ballroom of Netherfield. "What I won't do for a friend."

Chapter 2: Elizabeth

Dawn broke and despite having been up until the wee hours, Elizabeth always rose with the sun. Knowing no one else would be up yet, she determined to dress quickly and make her way to Oakham Mount. However, this morning something felt… different. It took her a moment to realize she was not in her room. "Oh my goodness! Where am I? How did I get here?" Panicked, she wanted to scream but quickly thought better of it. What if she had been kidnapped? She didn't want to draw attention to herself. Quietly rising from the very plush bed - far better than hers at home - she decided to look around.

The room was very masculine, mostly dark wood paneling and forest green linens of very high quality. Then she saw them, men's clothing laid out as if the owner were to come in any moment to dress. She spun around to make sure she was alone. It would not do to be in a man's room alone, much less in only her night shift. Wait? This is not my night shift, this is a man's nightshirt. Why am I in men's clothing? Her head was pounding. What was going on? Did I drink too much wine last night? I only had one glass of wine with dinner. Perhaps someone spiked the punch?

Deciding that she needed more sleep, Elizabeth crawled back into the large, exquisite bed. Reaching for the covers to pull over her head, she stopped. Her hands looked wrong, manly even. She felt her face… stubble. Her hair was shorter, only just to her collar. She ran to the mirror, saw *his* reflection, screamed, and - for the first time in her life - fainted.

She awoke again surrounded by Mr. Bingley, a man Bingley referred to as Davies, and a footman. "Darcy! What happened? Are you alright?" Bingley asked with the utmost concern. "Shall we call the doctor?"

Elizabeth sat up, utterly confused. How has this happened? *WHY* had this happened?

"Mr. Darcy, Sir, I don't think you ought to get up." Davies protested as Elizabeth pulled herself off the ground.

"No, No. I am… fine. I am not sure what happened. I... I …"

"You screamed like a woman and then we found you out cold on the ground!" Bingley said with a small chuckle seeing that his old friend was going to be alright.

Attempting to cover up her rising panic and not let on that she was in fact a *she,* Elizabeth merely grumbled, "I did not scream like a woman. I slipped and must have hit my head." Why did doing anything 'like a woman' have to be an insult? I bet they couldn't have a baby 'like a woman!' she thought to herself.

"Well, then I will leave you with Davies to get dressed." Bingley said turning toward the door. "I'll see you downstairs for breakfast. Now that I am up so early, we should go for a ride before the others wake up."

Fresh panic arose. While it was true that Elisabeth was no horsewoman, she knew she certainly was not the accomplished rider Mr. Darcy surely was. Thinking fast, Elizabeth fairly squeaked, "Um, I'm not sure I should with my headache. Another time?" It sounded weak even to her but Bingley seemed to take her at her word.

"Yes, of course, I should have realized." And with that she was left alone with Davies who was apparently Mr. Darcy's valet. Despite the realization that Davies only saw Mr. Darcy when he looked at her, she could not help being self-conscious. She turned her back to the mirror to avoid seeing more of Mr. Darcy's nakedness than was absolutely necessary and refused to look down while getting dressed.

However hard she tried to preserve Mr. Darcy's modesty as well as her own, the fates had conspired against her for it was not but a few minutes before she realized she had to use the loo. Excusing herself, she made her way into the privy and stood there for a few minutes, trying to decide what to do. "Do I take off the pants entirely and have to redress? Do I open the front flap of his breeches and thereby have to touch… *him*?" She decided on removing the pants. That way she could avoid touching any private areas directly by sitting and then redressing with care.

Once that was done, she straightened her clothing with some help from a disapproving Davies, and headed down to breakfast.

"Ah, there you are! Feeling better? You look a bit out of sorts." Bingley said looking concerned but nevertheless filling his plate with what appeared to be a second helping of most everything.

Trying to act as she believed Mr. Darcy would (how would he act when it was just he and Mr. Bingley?), she walked to the sideboard and began to fill her plate. Taking twice what she normally would, she sat down across from Bingley. "I feel much better, Mr.... uh, Charles, thank you." Quickly changing the subject, she added, "You appeared to enjoy yourself last night."

Judging by the surprised look on his face, she had clearly caught Bingley off guard with the statement. Perhaps men did not talk about these things like women did. How odd. Before she thought much more of it, Bingley began, "Darcy, she is an Angel! I know you tire of hearing it but I mean it this time. Jane Bennet is all that is good and lovely!'

Tire of hearing it? Why would he tire of hearing it? Jane is good and lovely. Ooohhhh, realizing suddenly that Bingley must speak of Jane in these terms quite often, she sighed happily.

However, Bingley mistook her happy sigh for one of resignation at best and so added, "Now I know you say you cannot tell whether or not she truly likes *me* or is just following

Mrs. Bennet's direction, but I tend to disagree. I think I detect a real preference." Quietly adding, "At least, I think I do."

Anger burned within Elizabeth! How could Mr. Darcy say such ridiculous things? OF COURSE Jane truly preferred Mr. Bingley! She is shy! However, she could not come right out and say that. How on Earth would Mr. Darcy explain this sudden change of heart and better understanding of the feelings of a woman he did not really know very well? No matter, she must endeavor to reassure Mr. Bingley of Jane's affections as best she could under the circumstances.

"Charles, I watched the two of you last night and I think I can now say that Miss Bennet may have true affection for you that is merely covered by an innate shyness. She may - in fact - be guarding her heart as many young ladies are taught." Seeing the smile spread across Bingley's face, she knew her words were having the desired effect.

"You know, Darce, I think you may be correct. Miss Bennet does have a certain shyness about her until she is truly comfortable around someone. In that regard, you two are alike."

Before she could respond, Caroline walked in and all conversation about Jane Bennet abruptly ceased.

Chapter 3: Darcy

Darcy, not one to sleep in, awoke early but with a blinding headache. He *had* imbibed in too much wine last night due to his frustration with what he was now referring to as the 'Bennet Situation'. It had become quite clear to him that not only was Charles in great danger of making an imprudent match but the longer he stayed in Hertfordshire, he was as well. Elizabeth Bennet was more beguiling every day. Her wit, intelligence, her willingness to challenge him, combined with what could only be described as a very pleasing (although petite) figure drew him further in every time he met her.

So, rather than rising before the rest of the household, he did something he almost never did (and was sure he'd never hear the end of) he went back to sleep. A few hours later, he woke to the sound of a familiar voice - and not a pleasant one - just outside his door. However, try as he might, he could not place it. Opening his eyes, light flooding the room, he instantly realized he was NOT at Netherfield! Sitting bolt upright in bed he saw *her* reflection in the mirror across the small room.

In the name of all that was good and holy, Elizabeth Bennet's reflection stared back at him and she was in only her night shift with her hair was falling from a loose braid down, around her shoulders. Other than the confused look on her face, she looked exactly how he imagined she would (although he never thought to see her in this state *here at Longbourn).* He reached his hand up to touch her cheek and groaned. Her skin was so soft. Elizabeth's reflection made the same movements. Standing, he walked to the mirror and stood there, staring at her. He often stared at her but never so openly. Without meaning to, he noticed that the buttons of her shift had come undone in the night and he could easily make out the swell of her breasts before suddenly realizing to his horror that he was essentially intruding on her privacy and he quickly put on the robe that lay at the foot of her bed. Elizabeth would rightly be furious with him if she knew he had taken even that smallest liberty and he was for the first time in recent memory ashamed that he had let his mind wander so far in that direction.

Darcy was nothing if not practical and though he could not understand his current situation he began to ponder all daily activities that would require a breach of her privacy and in return, his privacy by her – for she must be similarly… displaced, mustn't she?. He colored at the thought of her having to dress him, bathe him, and all those activities that were essential but not something one wanted to be witnessed doing. He also began to think on the physical differences each would encounter being suddenly thrown into the body of a member of the opposite sex. For instance, he was certain getting dressed today would require him to put on very intimate apparel. What if he is not returned to his body before her womanly time occurs this month (oh, please don't let that be the case). How was he to get back into his own body? How did this occur? What if Elizabeth was not in his body but someone else was? And how was he to find out? How could he behave as Elizabeth normally would when he was not acquainted with these aspects of her life? He had no idea how women spoke amongst each other. He could not embroider or paint. As luck would have it, he was musical but not on the same instruments - and though he loved to hear Elizabeth sing - even he would admit to having better technique due to regular practice with Georgiana.

"Georgiana! What will I do about her guardianship? I trust Elizabeth to make the best decisions she can but there is much she is unaware of and Georgiana is *MY* sister! That settles it, I must find Elizabeth as soon as I reasonably can without drawing suspicion. In the meantime, how am I to get dressed?"

As if summoned by her innate understanding that someone was in need, Jane knocked at the door.

"Good morning, Lizzy. You are not dressed! If you don't hurry all the strawberry tarts that Hill made will be gone and I know how you love her tarts!"

With an almost audible sigh of relief, he allowed Jane to pick out a day dress that only required a relatively simple girdle and pantaloons - for which he was much relieved. However, despite his best effort, he was also quite aroused by the whole exercise and was very glad that the only noticeable physical evidence of this was his face and neck being flushed. If Jane noticed anything amiss, she said nothing and they were soon downstairs, joining the others to break their fast.

As predicted, it had taken longer than usual to make himself presentable and by the time they had joined the others, the strawberry tarts were indeed, gone. However, the many other choices left nothing to be desired (Darcy actually preferred lemon tarts anyway) and he sat down at the only place left at the table.

Chapter 4: Elizabeth

After breaking their fast, Bingley decided that it was only appropriate to call on his nearest neighbors, the Bennets, to discuss the ball. In truth, he could not resist the chance that he may be able to take Miss Bennet out for a walk with Darcy and Miss Elizabeth acting as chaperones Since Elizabeth was desperate to see Darcy and discover if he was in the same situation as she was, she made no objections. Perhaps then they could figure out how to reverse whatever curse they had fallen under.

Upon arriving at Longbourn, Bingley stepped out of the carriage. Elizabeth briefly hesitated before stepping down, waiting for the footman to offer his hand before quickly realizing how odd it would appear for the towering Mr. Darcy to wait for assistance from a carriage. It took but a moment before they were shown into the parlor and Elizabeth's eyes immediately sought out Mr. Darcy's. How odd to see her person standing across the room, knowing that to everyone else's eyes, she appeared to be Mr. Darcy. She also noticed that while Mr. Darcy was appropriately dressed, he had hastily arranged her hair and she was immediately embarrassed that anyone should see her in such disarray.

After several minutes of small talk, Bingley suggested a walk to Meryton. Mr. Collins was suffering from 'an upset stomach' and decided to stay 'home'. Upon hearing this, Mary begged off citing her need to practice on the piano forte but Kitty and Lydia immediately agreed and begged to call at Lucas Lodge to see their friend, Mariah. So it was that they all set out to Meryton together. However, it did not take long for them to pair off with Kitty and Lydia in the lead, Jane and Mr. Bingley next, followed - at some distance - by Elizabeth and Darcy.

As soon as he was certain that their conversation could not be overheard, Mr. Darcy turned to Elizabeth, "How did this happen? As soon as you and Bingley walked into the parlor, I knew it was you, but… how can you be in my body and I in yours?"

Sighing heavily, half in relief and have exasperation, Elizabeth replied, "I do not know! I have never heard of such a thing? Have you?"

"No. I have not. Which means I have no idea how to switch us back. Nor how long we might stay… like this." After a few moments of awkward silence he added, "I know not how to broach this subject as we shall both be fairly mortified but I feel it best to set ground rules for our conduct when in public and…err... in private."

Blushing from the top of *his* head to the tips of *his toes*, Elizabeth agreed that such rules must be set as much as possible.

However, while she was certain he had not meant to imply she would engage in any inappropriate behavior, she could not be completely sure. "Of course! There are likely certain expectations that people have regarding our behavior and it would not do to fail to meet those expectations out of ignorance. For example, only my family and very dear friends call me 'Lizzy'. I would never give a new acquaintance leave to call me anything but Miss Elizabeth or Elizabeth (even if we feel a kinship quickly)."

"I am generally called 'Darcy' by my close friends and Mr. Darcy by everyone else."

"Surely your family doesn't call you 'Darcy'!" Elizabeth could not help but chuckle a bit at the thought.

"Well no, to be sure. My family calls me 'Fitzwilliam' but since my cousin is Col. Fitzwilliam, it can be a bit confusing." As if reading her confused expression - and wondering if that is how his face looked when *he* was confused - he clarified, "Fitzwilliam was my mother's maiden name and it is tradition for daughters to pass it along to their first born sons."

Looking around, Elizabeth realized they were over halfway to Meryton where they would no longer be able to speak privately. Deciding it was now or never, Elizabeth brought up the topic she dreaded most but also most needed to have settled. "Mr. Darcy, it is likely already apparent to you from having to get dressed this morning, that there are a number of rather… intimate situations which may arise. Let us agree that we will each act with the utmost regard for the privacy of the other without making absurd requests regarding particular behaviors. For example, I have changed many a diaper in my time and have had to bathe male babies…" Darcy laughed uncomfortably at this part of her speech. "While I know you are not a small child, I will endeavor to treat your body with the indifferent respect I would my nephews', knowing that we are all made as we are for a purpose." There that wasn't so hard to say. She refused to acknowledge to herself that it would not be so easy for Mr. Darcy considering female babes are not developed as a woman her age is. The mere thought of him having to handle her body - even for innocent purposes - made her blush profusely.

"Miss Elizabeth?"

"Hmm?"

"May I ask you something that would normally be none of my business?"

"I should think so. I have a myriad of questions myself."

"Do you have a beau... whose attentions I will be expected to receive with pleasure?"

Elizabeth laughed openly and was momentarily shocked to hear Mr. Darcy's deep baritone come from her laughter. Remembering their situation, she realized *he* may have someone as well. "No, sir. I do not. Do you? Not a beau but… Miss Bingley perhaps?"

Mr. Darcy stopped walking causing Elizabeth to stop and look at him seriously. 'My goodness, it is still so strange to see myself standing there, looking back at me.' "I'm sorry. I do not mean to pry," she continued.

Mr. Darcy, who until just now thought that Miss Elizabeth was aware of his growing attraction had been quite literally stopped in his tracks by her question. "No, Miss Elizabeth, I am in NO way attached or attracted to Miss Bingley in spite of (and in fact, perhaps *because* of) her throwing herself in my path as often as possible. To be honest, you must be on your guard with Miss Bingley. She is not above a compromise and I cannot be trapped into a marriage with her! Please, Miss Elizabeth, guard my reputation as I will guard yours."

His earnest plea touched her heart and she promised him that she would do everything in her power to maintain the polite but distant relationship he had so carefully cultivated. She also noted that she felt a small measure of relief at his denial of any attachments. But that was a subject she would think upon later, if she chose to.

Resuming their walk, Elizabeth took up the conversation again, "Let us meet tomorrow morning, early, with a list of important information and issues which need to be addressed. That way we can try our best to be prepared. I gathered this morning that my being up so early was not a surprise to those at Netherfield. Do you always maintain country hours?"

"Yes, I do. Although I woke up late this morning and it was noted by your entire family. I will have to be more careful in the future… until we figure this out, that is."

It was at this point that they realized that the rest of the party had slowed to allow them to catch up because they were just entering the outskirts of Meryton. It would not be prudent to allow any rumors to begin by being seen walking in pairs rather than as a large party.

Chapter 5: Elizabeth

Their trip into Meryton consisted of stopping at several shops for the younger Bennet sisters to peruse the newly arrived ribbons on their way to Elizabeth's aunt Philips' house where they were to return a pattern book that Mrs. Bennet had recently borrowed. While waiting for Kitty, Lydia, and Mariah to finalize their purchases, Mr. Darcy noticed the bookstore across the street. In his best attempt to sound like Miss Elizabeth, he spoke up. "Jane, Mr. Bingley, Mr. Darcy, would you think me terribly rude if I stepped into the bookstore across the street?"

Jane responded a bit surprised but with no small amusement, "Lizzy, you were just there two days ago. You know Mr. Townsend won't have any new books for a few weeks."

Bingley quickly jumped in, "Darcy, weren't you looking for a book in my library the other day? You ought to accompany Miss Elizabeth and ask about it. What book was that again? Something or other of poetry, I believe."

Elizabeth was caught unaware and having no reply for Bingley's question made a valiant attempt. "Yes, of course! It was the latest volume of Wordsworth I believe." Turning to Miss Elizabeth, she offered his arm, "Shall we?"

Darcy seemed both surprised and embarrassed by the gesture which would have been an appropriate response to the situation as is but seeing his reaction made her realize that while the real Mr. Darcy would likely have accompanied her to the bookstore, he would not likely have offered his arm. However, it mattered not as both Charles and Jane were already engrossed in their own conversation and had not appeared to notice.

Crossing the street, Elizabeth and Darcy entered the bookstore. It was not as large as he was used to but they were immediately greeted by Mr. Townsend who was always happy to see Elizabeth and was hopeful of making a large sale when seeing Mr. Darcy. Next to Mr. Townsend was his daughter, Lucy-Anne. Lucy-Anne was two years older than Elizabeth but blushed like a school-girl when she saw Darcy enter the store. Elizabeth mentally rolled her eyes.

Elizabeth quietly whispered to Mr. Darcy, "Ask him how Mrs. Townsend is faring and if her headaches have abated since she has been in Bath. The other day when I was here he told me she was to be away for another two weeks."

"Right, thank you." He whispered in return. Then turning from the shelf he had been searching, he repeated Elizabeth's question exactly, hoping to sound natural. It must have worked for Mr. Townsend looked fondly at *her* and answered, "Oh Miss Elizabeth, you are too kind! She is much improved. So much so, that I fear she may want to stay!" While he said this with a smile, Elizabeth and Darcy could tell the older gentlemen clearly thought there may be something to it. "I may have to bring in my nephew to help me run the store. But, I am getting older... It might be nice to take a step back from the day to day." As if remembering that he had customers, Mr. Townsend looked up and smiled. "Forgive an old man for rambling. How can I help you today?"

This time Elizabeth spoke up. "I am looking to help Mr. Bingley stock his library. Miss Elizabeth was telling me that last week you received a shipment of some of the latest works of Keats, Byron, and Wordsworth. I should like to take a look." After a moment she added, "I am also looking for a book on crop rotation that Mr. Bennet mentioned to me only this morning."

With that, Mr. Townsend's smile grew and he made his way around the counter to assist Mr. Darcy in finding the new arrivals. Once he left them alone, Darcy turned to Elizabeth to see her smiling widely. She knew full well that while this sale would be a large one for Mr. Townsend, the cost would mean nothing to Mr. Darcy and so he acquiesced to the purchase. "You do realize that I already own a few of these books, including - I believe - the one you mentioned on crop rotation. It was particularly insightful but not so much that I would normally purchase a second copy," he said to her - amusement obvious in his voice.

In her typically arch manner - and not at all resembling Darcy - she replied, "Well as I said, these are to be a gift for Mr. Bingley. Except the one on crop rotation; that one I will keep and read myself before leaving it for him to read when he has the time."

Clearly surprised, Mr. Darcy whispered, "*You* enjoy reading about crop rotation?" At that moment, Mr. Townsend walked up with a suggested book for Elizabeth and hearing *her* remark interjected, "My dear, no one *enjoys* reading about crop rotation but men like Mr. Darcy have a responsibility to keep abreast of the latest techniques that could improve their yield. Is that not so?"

Elizabeth coughed to cover her very unmanly impulse to giggle, "Quite right. I find that improving the means of production often leads not only to improved output, but also improved morale for my tenants. For, in the end, I would be master of nothing if my tenants were not willing to work for me."

Darcy was impressed by how similar her opinions were to his own and the fact that she took an interest at all. However, it was dangerous for her to profess her opinions when speaking as him. Seeming to read his thoughts, and seeking a safer topic Elizabeth changed the subject back to books that might be purchased as a gift for Netherfield's library. Elizabeth mentally chastised herself and resolved to be more careful when speaking as everyone else would attribute her words to Mr. Darcy and that could have undesirable consequences.

Leaving the bookstore with one new book in hand and several to be delivered, Elizabeth and Darcy stepped out into the street. Darcy took this opportunity before they reached Jane and Bingley to say, "We are fortunate, Miss Elizabeth, you and I seem to be of such similar attitudes when it comes to *my* role as master of an estate." Smiling to reassure her when he noticed color rising upon *his* cheeks (seeing himself blush was quite uncomfortable but so was knowing that she had taken his words as an admonishment), he smiled again and added, "I wonder, how have you come by such progressive notions? It is uncommon for ladies to be involved in the management of an estate; does your father encourage you in this interest? "My father has always encouraged *all* my interests. I have free use of his library, which holds quite an eclectic collection."

"Might I ask as to your education? That is, I may be expected to know certain things but not others." In truth, Elizabeth Bennet was becoming more fascinating by the minute. He had never known a woman to take an interest in agriculture, but he was sure that was not the most unusual thing about her.

"I have studied Philosophy, History, Politics, Maths, and - of course - languages."

At this, Mr. Darcy smiled widely (which Elizabeth thought must be how she appeared most often and was pleased that his smiling did not appear to change the effect on her face. She had always thought her smile was the one physical feature that she could take pride in and regularly displayed to her advantage). "Ah, parlez vous francais, mademoiselle?"

Returning the smile she replied, "Oui Monsieur! Je parle francais, hablo español, and I can read Greek. Although," she admitted sheepishly, "I only took on the latter because then I could read some of the more risqué stories from mythology without my mother chastising me."

"Well then, you must take Hector for a ride sometime. While he is strong and intimidating in appearance, he is an excellent mount for both hunting and riding."

"I'm afraid I am no horsewoman, Mr. Darcy."

"That may be problematic as I am most definitely a horse*man."* Rubbing the back of *her* neck in a manner he usually did when he was thinking, he realized that he had yearned to graze his fingers gently over her skin and marveled that he could do so now in a most innocent gesture and no one would bat an eyelash. However, he also realized that this was an unladylike gesture and quickly brought her hand away from her neck. "Hmm, I will think on this tonight and we can discuss it when we meet tomorrow."

"Yes, I have already avoided a ride with Mr. Bingley this morning by claiming I felt unwell after I fainted this morning."

"You fainted? I have never fainted in my life!" Sighing loudly, "Bingley will think I have become missish." After recollecting himself, he hastily sought to ensure that Elizabeth had, indeed, fully recovered from her ordeal. She assured him she was well and they both chuckled a little.

Elizabeth - with her signature, arch smile that Darcy was sure no one had ever seen on his face before - teased, "Really? You have never fainted? I would not have guessed that." Then she turned and walked in the direction of the others leaving Darcy to determine if she thought him a dandy.

Chapter 6: Darcy

The rest of the day was uneventful until it was time to prepare for bed. Darcy, once again, had no idea what to do and could only rely upon the basic knowledge that came with being the guardian of his younger sister. However, even that was lacking as he had relied heavily upon Mrs. Reynolds to perform many of the motherly duties on Georgiana behalf.

'Start with the dress and then the hair. That should be safe enough.' He began by removing the dress itself which left him in a girdle and petticoat. To help ensure Elizabeth's privacy, Darcy again turned away from any mirrors and looked at the ceiling as much as possible. Taking delight in Elizabeth's nakedness would be uncouth. 'I may look like Elizabeth, but I am still a gentleman.' Once he had successfully changed into her night shift, he put on her robe, and sat down at the vanity to unpin and brush her hair.

Taking out one pin at a time, Darcy relished the feel of the soft curls falling down around her neck. He ran his hands gently through them and even pulled one forward to take in Elizabeth's perfume of lavender and rose water. 'My goodness this is going to be torture.'

Jane knocked on the door and entered quietly, already changed and ready for bed as well. Darcy noted that seeing Jane in her night clothes had not stirred up any feelings of desire within him and yet, the mere thought of Elizabeth (much more so this current situation) did. He wanted to possess Elizabeth's body in a very different way than he currently was. And more than that, he wanted her to desire the same.

"Lizzy, you are very far away this evening. I wonder what - or who - can be occupying your mind so?" Jane was not one to pry but she had noticed the marked attention Mr. Darcy had paid to her sister this afternoon and the fact that this time, Elizabeth had seemly accepted his attentions. "Have you decided Mr. Darcy is not so very bad after all? I have long thought you two were more similar than you realized."

Taken aback, Darcy took a moment to collect his thoughts. 'Why would Elizabeth have *disliked* me? I can think of no offense I have given her...' Then it hit him - the assembly! She must have heard his foolish, untrue remarks. 'Oh no, how I foolish I have been. I have been laboring under the apprehension that Miss Elizabeth would have welcomed my suit only to find out, now when I am actually considering her, that she had never intended to attract my attention at all!' Somehow, as much as this disheartened him, it made him more secure in the fact that Elizabeth would not welcome his attentions for his money. *If* he could win her over, it would be that she had come to respect - perhaps someday even love - him.

"Jane, you make too much of a simple walk and some shared interests. Perhaps Mr. Darcy is not *as* bad as I once believed but that does not excuse his previous poor behavior. I will proceed in an effort to be friendly. After all, I believe Mr. Bingley is likely to call on you often and Mr. Darcy will probably accompany him. It would not do to be uncivil."

Darcy decided that not everything about this odd situation was bad. Perhaps in speaking with Jane, he could ascertain her true feelings for his friend. He was not sure how he would relay that information if it became necessary but it would be valuable to have nonetheless.

"Jane, you may tease me about Mr. Darcy but you cannot deny that Mr. Bingley seems to enjoy spending time with *you*."

Jane sat on the bed and sighed heavily - a wistful sigh that attested to her dreamlike state - "Oh Lizzy, he is the most amiable man of my acquaintance. He is kind and thoughtful…"

Interrupting, he added, "And rich…"

"Oh phooey, you sound like mama! You know I'd think him the best of men if he were as poor as a church mouse. I will admit, I don't want to be poor but I would not turn away true respect and affection for a lack of funds. Nor would you, Lizzy! But I believe you almost refuse to see the possibilities before you *because* you are prejudiced against wealth."

This thought struck Darcy with force. Would Elizabeth hold his wealth *against* him? He had never considered it. How would Elizabeth respond to this? "I will not pretend that I do not believe that those of great wealth often display an air of pride and even disdain that would be unfounded if not for their elevated status but I am not so foolish as to refuse the attentions of a man based *solely* on his situation in life. After all, I would hope to judge people on their merits."

"Most often, Lizzy, you do but in the case of Mr. Darcy, I believe you attribute his actions to motives that may not be his."

Curious now, he could not help but ask her to elaborate.

"For instance, you have often said that you believe Mr. Darcy stares at you only to find fault. I would suggest that perhaps he stares at you because he admires you."

Darcy was flooded with a mixture of emotions, not the least of which was embarrassment. He has thought his 'staring' was merely stealing a glance occasionally and certainly not enough to be noted by others. But he was also disheartened to know that Elizabeth had thought him to be finding fault. What was there to find fault with? Attempting to end the conversation, he simply said, "Perhaps." Yawning, he added, "Goodnight, Jane."

Yawning herself, Jane bid her sister goodnight and left the room to dream of a future she could only hope for with a certain gentleman from Netherfield.

Chapter 7: Elizabeth

The next morning dawned clear and crisp. Under normal circumstances, Elizabeth would be beyond excited for her morning walk. However, today she had agreed to meet Mr. Darcy so could he teach her to ride because no one would believe that he had suddenly developed an aversion for the sport if she refused. So, she had reluctantly ordered Henry, the young stable boy to have Hector readied for an early morning ride thus ensuring there would be few witnesses to her clumsy attempts to make it away from Netherfield in the direction of Oakham Mount.

While Elizabeth was quite well versed in *how* to ride, she had not been on a horse since she had been thrown at age 7. She had spent some weeks with her arm in a wooden splint, drinking chamomile tea and other herbs to reduce the pain due to the nasty fall. Occasionally, her mother would allow her a teaspoon of brandy if the pain became too much for her but her father staunchly refused Laudanum - a fact she hated at the time but had been grateful for in the long-run.

Despite understanding the methods of riding, Elizabeth was still very anxious. To further complicate matters, she would have to ride astride Hector and not side-saddle. Would that be better or worse? She hoped better.

Gathering her courage, she called for Davies to help her dress. Looking in the mirror, she had to admit that Mr. Darcy cut a fine figure in his riding attire. Davies would clearly not stand for his master to be less than immaculately dressed and so his breeches were of a fine quality that had not been worn often as they had not stretched in the slightest but, rather, fit like new. Additionally, she could not help but smile at how often Davies must be frustrated in his attempts to tame Darcy's rather unruly curls for she often saw Darcy run his hands through them when he appeared uncomfortable and wondered if Davies cursed this unconscious act.

Unable to delay her departure any longer, she set out for the stables. The sun was rising just over the trees and magnificent pinks and oranges colored the sky. This was Elizabeth's favorite time of year. Leaves were changing color but the bitter cold of winter had not yet set in. Days were still long enough to enjoy out of doors and with the harvest over, more people were free to do so.

Entering the stable, she saw Hector being tended to by Henry. He was no fewer than 16-17 hands which made him incredibly intimidating but less so, since she realized, with Mr. Darcy's height, she could still see over Hector's back. Slowly approaching, she removed an apple slice from her pocket. "There are more where that came from if you behave."

She noticed Henry giving her an odd look. "Mr. Darcy, Sir. I know you didn't specifically say to but I went ahead and gave Hector some extra oats and carrots like you usually do. I didn't know yous gonna be bringing apples, Sir. I didn't mean to spoil his appetite."

Henry was a boy of 12 and while he was young, he was an attentive hand and a quick learner, and rather large for his age. Elizabeth had known him since he was a baby but she couldn't very well say anything about that now. She noticed that while he appeared apologetic, he did not seem afraid. That spoke highly of how Mr. Darcy had likely treated him in the past. She found herself to be unexpectedly gratified by this.

Elizabeth led Hector out of the stable to the side on which trees obscured the view from the house. Putting one foot into the stir up, she lifted herself off the ground. Taking only a moment to consider how, she determined to throw her leg across the beast and end up astride the animal like she had seen her father do many times. To her amazement, she found the task to be quite easily accomplished. Wearing breeches allowed for an ease of movement which she had not accounted for. With that done, she realized Hector was rather anxious to begin. "Patience big fella, I'm afraid you'll have to go slow with me." Then fearing she may be overheard, she hastily added, "I hit my head yesterday and don't want to cause my head to ache as it did."

Fortunately, Elizabeth was familiar with the landscape and knew what paths to take and which to avoid. After a short time she crossed onto Longbourn lands where she found Mr. Darcy sitting on a felled log, reading a book. 'Hmm, he does a rather good job impersonating me,' she thought to herself. 'No one would know by looking that anything was amiss.'

"Good morning," she called out to him.

He looked up and a smile crossed his face. "Good morning! I thought this was to be a riding lesson but you seem to have mastered the art already!"

With a self-deprecating laugh she replied, "Hardly Sir. I am able to stay atop this fine animal because he is being merciful. Though I think the apple slices I used to bribe him may have helped." Lowering her voice conspiratorially she added, "However, I think he *knows*. He is not altogether sure how to react to me. I look like you but I am sure I do not act enough like you to be convincing. Animals have a sense about these things."

Darcy thought about this for a moment and stroking Hector's strong neck in a familiar gesture, said, "He likely feels your apprehension. That, and I usually give him carrots." He smiled before continuing, "No matter. We will have you galloping soon enough. Although I must admit, it is strange seeing Hector - quite literally - through your eyes. I can see how being this petite would cause you to be intimidated."

Dismounting with ease (once again due to the breeches), Elizabeth reached into her saddle bag. Taking out two biscuits and some fruit she offered some to Darcy, "Before we ride… let us break our fast. I, for one, am famished from my adventure here."

In response to her words, Darcy's stomache grumbled. "That sounds delightful. Thank you."

They sat upon the tree that Darcy previously occupied.

"Mr. Darcy, I find that since… becoming you, I grow immensely hungry. And then when I do eat, I eat three times as much as usual. I sincerely hope I do not make you fat!" she said laughing between bites.

"Really? I find I am unable to eat very much at one sitting! I have twice filled my plate with far more than I was able to eat and received more than one admonishing look from your mother."

"Oh dear, I fear Lydia likely made a comment or two as well? I hope you were not offended."

"Actually, it was Mr. Collins who commented - although I believe Lydia's comment would have been cleverer. He rather bluntly informed me that his patroness, Lady Catherine de Bourgh (my aunt, incidentally) would not approve of a woman taking such large portions. It implies she is lowborn."

"That man is insufferable! I should be able to eat as much as I choose in my own home! I loathe him." she vented to no one in particular.

"Mr. Collins is quite persistent in his attentions to you, Miss Elizabeth. To be honest, under the circumstances, it is quite uncomfortable." He said this with pitiful look attempting to make her laugh at his discomfort. Much to his relief it worked and she smiled. He continued, "I am relieved to hear that you do not welcome his attentions but I am unsure how to proceed. It seems your mother is very keen on the match and I do not want to cause a rift by rebuffing him, nor do I want to encourage him - from a personal standpoint."

"While my mother does desire the match due to the entail, my father will back my decision to refuse Mr. Collins if he is foolish enough to propose."

"Entail? So he is the beneficiary? And yet you would refuse a man who - granted he is 'insufferable' - could provide security for you and your family?"

He said this is a most unassuming and gentle manner so Elizabeth decided to answer him honestly. "Only the deepest love and respect for a man could tempt me to marry. I have seen the result of not respecting one's partner in life and I would rather be 'thrown out into hedgerows' than marry a man, like Collins, that I cannot respect."

"It is quite unusual to meet a person in society these days who does not place a higher value on material comfort than on the intangible comforts in life. It is... refreshing."

"I'm sure being both exceedingly handsome and rich you have had more than your share of match-making mama's and mercenary daughters." As soon as she said this he smiled, a large, Cheshire cat like smile. It was only then that she realized that she had admitted to finding him 'exceedingly handsome.'

She immediately colored and turned away to look at some imaginary bird or some such thing, hoping for a crack in the earth to appear and swallow her whole.

Her words and obvious embarrassment encouraged the hope that perhaps all was not lost and that he may still have a chance to win her affection. It had become clear to him that her good opinion meant more to him than he had been willing to admit. Attempting to ease her discomfort he teased, "Yes, well I do not know if I have ever looked better than I do in this blue muslin!"

Then seeing her laugh lightly, he added, "I have always thought it complemented the rose in your cheeks rather nicely." And just like that, she found herself blushing again.

Chapter 8: Elizabeth

In less time that she thought possible, Elizabeth found that she could comfortably walk, trot, and canter. However, she knew she must be able to gallop if she wanted to keep others from questioning Mr. Darcy's well-being. It was well known that the men of the Netherfield party enjoyed a good hunt. Elizabeth was an excellent shot but add the element of riding and she was not so sure, especially since she had not yet mastered the herculean task.

Looking down from atop Hector, she decided it was time to address her fear. "Mr. Darcy, I know the next step is to gallop but to be honest, I find my fear may be overcoming my courage."

Mr. Darcy looked down at the ground and for the first time in Elizabeth's memory seemed to fidget. "It takes time to become comfortable with speed and unfortunately time is one thing we do not have. However, I have an idea. I used to do this with Georgie when she was learning but I am afraid you may object... I can ride behind you until you feel secure and then you can try on your own. I know it is not usually done but I am afraid given the time constraint it may be necessary."

She smiled, "It is much less objectionable than falling off this horse. I have done that before and do not wish to repeat the experience!"

Understanding dawned, "So that is where your fear comes from?" He could picture Elizabeth as a fearless young lady, probably climbing trees and getting into all sorts of scrapes. The image warmed his heart and he began to picture what their children might look like. He stopped, '*their children?* 'Where had that thought come from? It is one thing to be smitten, quite another to jump to fatherhood.' He would have to guard his thoughts very carefully for he was not even sure yet if he would be able to win Miss Elizabeth's heart.

Leading Hector over to the fallen log, he prepared to mount the horse behind Miss Elizabeth. However, he quickly spied a problem. Feeling quite foolish, he shook his head. "It seems, Miss Elizabeth that I did not account for the difference in our sizes. Normally, *I* would be the larger of the two and so riding behind to help keep you secure while still steering the horse." Here he paused and let out a small chuckle, "But as you are the... larger one, I will not be able to see. So it seems that I will need to ride in front and you will have to reach around me to hold the reins (in case anyone happens by it will look to them as if *Mr. Darcy* is teaching *Miss Elizabeth* how to steer using the reins (that alone would have been scandalous).

Enjoying the somewhat confusing, circular logic at play, "Is that not almost exactly what is happening?"

As he mounted the horse in front of her, he just said, "I suppose it is." However, it only took a moment to realize he had yet another problem. He had never mounted a horse in a dress. This day was shaping up to be the most humiliating of his memory. "I would ask you to avert your eyes but I fail to see the point."

"Oh come now, Mr. Darcy," she teased mercilessly, "you are merely experiencing the ridiculous, daily hardships forced upon ladies by society. I, however, am immensely enjoying the freedom afforded by these breeches. I may take up wearing them to ride when we eventually switch back." Pausing, as the realization hit again that she had no idea how or when or even *if* they would switch back. "You do think we *will* switch back, don't you?"

By this time, Mr. Darcy had gotten situated upon Hector. He took her hand and pulled it around him, then gently caressed it, "Yes, Miss Elizabeth, I do. I think maybe we are supposed to learn something from this experience."

"What do you think we need to learn? From each other?"

"I am not at all sure. But I am sure it will come and when it does, we will each be better for it."

With that, he adjusted their positions and eased Hector into a trot. As soon as he was sure that Elizabeth felt comfortable, he sped up to a canter. Then after a few minutes, he asked, "Are you ready?"

She held on tightly, "Yes, Sir. I believe so."

As odd as it was to have their positions reversed, he still reveled in the fact that she was trusting him to help her over one of her greatest fears. "Then hold on tightly. We are headed for Oakham Mount.

They raced, although Elizabeth was quite certain they were not at full speed, across the fields and soon reached the base of the mount. As they ascended, Elizabeth realized she was no longer afraid. She trusted Mr. Darcy implicitly - at least on horseback. The knowledge that he had overcome her defenses and so quickly, was as unsettling as it was exciting and she began to feel a few nervous butterflies in her stomach at being so close to him. She instinctively began to loosen her grip but Mr. Darcy pulled her closer, saying, "We are almost there, Miss Elizabeth. It would not do for you to fall so close to our destination - and so far from home - as I am quite sure I would not be able to lift you if you were hurt." Though he said this in all seriousness, there was a jovial quality to his voice which relaxed her and she leaned a little more into him, allowing her grip on him to remain firm.

At the peak of Oakham Mount, they both took the opportunity to dismount and stretch. "The view from here is beautiful. I can see why this is a favorite retreat."

"Yes, it is." She sighed wistfully. Then reaching into her, or rather his, jacket breast pocket, she pulled out a folded sheet of paper. "Now, Mr. Darcy, I have my list of information regarding myself and my family that will make your stay at Longbourn easier. Did you bring yours?"

"I did." He instinctively reached for his breast pocket before remembering, "This blasted dress! I have a new respect for you ladies. Now where did I find that pocket earlier?"

Seeing the dignified Mr. Darcy search for her pockets had Elizabeth doubled over in laughter until… "Mr. Darcy, that dress does not have pockets."

Both colored, "Ah, yes. Now I remember. I had to put it, er… well." Reaching slightly into the bosom of her dress he retrieved the list. "Believe me, Miss Elizabeth, I took no pleasure in touching your person and did so as little as possible." At her almost insulted and confused look he clarified, "That is to say, I did not mean to enjoy it, er… I did so as quickly as humanly possible. I apologize if I have made you uncomfortable."

Feigning offense she teased, "No pleasure?" To see the Master of Pemberley so obviously flustered caused Elizabeth to laugh all the more. "Mr. Darcy, as we said once before, there are occasions in which we will each be compelled to handle the other's… person. I am sure you were completely honorable. Do not fret, let us take a look at each other's lists."

*****

"Are you quite serious with this list Mr. Darcy? These are all responsibilities you shoulder, even as a guest of Mr. Bingley?"

Confused, Darcy looked up from Elizabeth's rather extensive list to answer, "Every one. Is there something in particular that is troubling you?"

"No, not *one*, but the sheer volume is worrisome. I am not sure how I shall keep it all straight."

"Most of my responsibilities will be handled by my steward for now. I have already written to him to tell him I will be indisposed for the foreseeable future. I will need you to post the letter, of course, after you seal it. My seal is in the top drawer of the writing desk in my room at Netherfield."

"Oh, that was brilliant of you! Of course, I shall post it after luncheon. Sadly, I have no one who can help you shoulder my responsibilities. However, by comparison, they seem rather light. Are there any *you* had questions about?"

"Well, I do have a question but I am afraid it is not on the list."

"Certainly Sir, I am sure there are many things I have taken for granted and so did not address them."

"Thank you. I am wondering if there are any books in your father's library that are off limits to you. You see, I am hoping to find one on human anatomy. I think it may come in handy should I have questions about..." And here he became rather more uncomfortable, "Well, for example, if I were to be in need of information regarding… well many feminine... things." Darcy had barely been able to get the words out and had not made eye contact even once during his speech. Much to his surprise and to his great relief, Elizabeth seemed only marginally uncomfortable.

With an understanding and a reassuring smile, she calmly put his fears to rest. "No books are off limits, which may surprise you as you begin your search. However, I believe the book you may find most helpful is likely to be in Kitty or Lydia's room. It is a book my aunt Gardiner sent to Jane after my mother refused to tell her anything other than 'menstruation is God's curse upon women for tempting Adam with forbidden fruit'. It has been passed between us sisters ever since as the need arose. You can simply ask for 'the book' and they will know which one you mean. However, it will be some time before that knowledge will be necessary so let us pray that we are returned to our *normal selves* before then!"

"Now, let us discuss lighter subjects. Tell me more about Georgie. She sounds delightful." When they felt they absolutely must leave or a search might ensue, they mounted Hector once again and headed back to the field in which they had met. It had only been a little over two hours but each felt that they had grown infinitely closer. Before turning back toward Longbourn, Darcy handed Elizabeth another piece of paper. It was another letter. "Please do not read this until you are safely ensconced in my room, then burn it. It contains information about my dealings with Mr. Wickham which I feel is important for you to know since I have ascertained in my short time with your sisters that he is a great favorite among them. I intend to share this information with your father as well - telling him that it came from you, *Mr. Darcy* - so that he may decide how best to proceed.

I hope that upon reading it, you will understand my obvious disdain for him."

With that, he turned and walked in the direction of her home, leaving her to ride back to Netherfield alone.

Chapter 9: Darcy

This chapter contains parts of Mr. Collins' proposal from Pride & Prejudice. Sadly, I do not own any part of Jane Austen's work.

Darcy returned to Longbourn with a burgeoning hope for his future. A future that he was more and more confident included Miss Elizabeth Bennet. Walking in the door, he was immediately assailed by Mrs. Bennet's shrieks. "It is about time you returned! Mr. Collins has been waiting patiently to speak with you all morning, my dear! Come now, into the parlor with you."

As he was being pulled into the parlor, he was flooded with relief for his conversation with Elizabeth that morning. He *knew* what was about to occur… Mr. Collins - that grasping sycophant - was about to propose. To think that Mr. Collins actually believed he was worthy of such an intelligent, lively, clever woman. Bah! Darcy wasn't even sure if *HE* was worthy of her which, admittedly, was quite a reversal of his earlier opinion. Nevertheless, he was resolved to try to earn her love and respect.

Entering the parlor, he saw Mr. Collins standing by the fireplace. He took a step farther into the room, trying to determine the best place to sit that would allow for a quick retreat when he heard the door shut behind him. He was alone… with Mr. Collins; he shuddered at the thought.

Seeing Elizabeth, Collins' eyes lit up and he smiled an expectant smile. "Cousin Elizabeth, I am glad you have returned. Please join me," he said as he moved toward the settee which would just accommodate both of them. Darcy sighed but did as he was asked.

"You can hardly doubt the purport of my discourse, however your natural delicacy may lead you to dissemble; my attentions have been too marked to be mistaken. Almost as soon as I entered the house I singled you out as the companion of my future life. But before I am run away with by my feelings on this subject, perhaps it will be advisable for me to state my reasons for marrying -- and moreover for coming into Hertfordshire with the design of selecting a wife, as I certainly did."

The idea of Mr. Collins, with all his solemn composure, being run away with by his feelings, made [Darcy] so near laughing that [he] could not use the short pause he allowed in any attempt to stop him farther, and he continued:

``My reasons for marrying are, first, that I think it a right thing for every clergyman in easy circumstances (like myself) to set the example of matrimony in his parish. Secondly, that I am convinced it will add very greatly to my happiness; and thirdly -- which perhaps I ought to have mentioned earlier, that it is the particular advice and recommendation of the very noble lady whom I have the honour of calling patroness. Twice has she condescended to give me her opinion (unasked too!) on this subject; and it was but the very Saturday night before I left Hunsford -- between our pools at

quadrille, while Mrs. Jenkinson was arranging Miss de Bourgh's foot-stool, that she said, "Mr. Collins, you must marry. A clergyman like you must marry. -- Chuse properly, chuse a gentlewoman for my sake; and for your own, let her be an active, useful sort of person, not brought up high, but able to make a small income go a good way. This is my advice. Find such a woman as soon as you can, bring her to Hunsford, and I will visit her." Allow me, by the way, to observe, my fair cousin that I do not reckon the notice and kindness of Lady Catherine de Bourgh as among the least of the advantages in my power to offer. You will find her manners beyond anything I can describe; and your wit and vivacity I think must be acceptable to her, especially when tempered with the silence and respect which her rank will inevitably excite. Thus much for my general intention in favour of matrimony; it remains to be told why my views were directed to Longbourn instead of my own neighbourhood, where I assure you there are many amiable young women. But the fact is, that being, as I am, to inherit this estate after the death of your honoured father (who, however, may live many years longer), I could not satisfy myself without resolving to choose a wife from among his daughters, that the loss to them might be as little as possible, when the melancholy event takes place -- which, however, as I have already said, may not be for several years. This has been my motive, my fair cousin, and I flatter myself it will not sink me in your esteem. And now nothing remains for me but to assure you in the most animated language of the violence of my affection. To fortune I am perfectly indifferent, and shall make no demand of that nature on your father, since I am well aware that it could not be complied with; and that one thousand pounds in the 4 per cents, which will not be yours till after your mother's decease, is all that you may ever be entitled to. On that head, therefore, I shall be uniformly silent; and you may assure yourself that no ungenerous reproach shall ever pass my lips when we are married."

By this time Darcy had heard quite enough! How dare this unworthy buffoon insult Miss Elizabeth so while proclaiming his violent affection. The uncomfortable thought that these had also been his own objections once upon a time, refused to fully surface. It did, nevertheless, niggle away in the back of his mind, leaving him more than a little ashamed of his previous attitude. *It was absolutely necessary to interrupt him now.*

With perhaps more compassion than he felt, Darcy attempted to respond as Elizabeth might - politely. "Sir, I thank you for the compliment you pay me, however I must decline." With that, Darcy made to stand and leave the parlor to hide away in Elizabeth's room. However, no sooner had he gotten to his feet than did he feel Mr. Collins firmly grab his wrist to forcibly prevent his escape.

Without thought, Darcy simply reacted. "Unhand me, Sir!"

Collins flustered and let go but persisted in his attempts to keep Elizabeth in his company. Stepping in front of her, he stammered, "I am aware *that it is usual with young ladies to reject the addresses of the man whom they secretly mean to accept, when he first applies for their favour; and that sometimes the refusal is repeated a second or even a third time."*

Aghast, Darcy simply stood and looked at Collins with an appraising eye. How could *he* be this self-assured? This toad of a man had not only proposed (an insult in itself) but now he refused to accept rejection. If a man ever spoke to Georgie this way, he would not be held accountable for his actions. Darcy would not allow this unacceptable speech to continue.

"Mr. Collins, I am not one of those ladies who would toy with a man's affections, hoping to encourage his pursuit! You must accept this as my final word, I do not love you and I will not marry you."

With that, Darcy left the room, verily barreling into Mrs. Bennet, Kitty, and Lydia who had been listening at the door as he strode determinedly past. Before he made it up the stairs, chaos erupted. Mr. Collins finally seemed to realize he might have been rejected, Mrs. Bennet was hollering after Elizabeth to come back downstairs, while Kitty and Lydia burst into uncontrollable laughter.

Once in Elizabeth's room, Darcy flopped onto the bed in a most unladylike manner. "Insufferable man is right!" Just then, Jane quietly knocked as she entered the room.

"Lizzy? Are you alright?"

Sweet, gentle Jane. She really was consistently serene. Darcy knew now that Jane would not easily show her feelings for she was so used to hiding them. He supposed someone had to be the voice of reason in this otherwise turbulent home. Lizzy was many things - many of which he had come to admire - but she was not always reasonable. Jane had fulfilled that role.

"Yes, Jane. I am. I cannot believe that mother *wants* me to marry him! We do not suit at all. I am convinced we would only make each other miserable. Does that not matter?"

"Of course, in time, mother will see that. She is just so worried that if something happens to Papa…"

Interrupting, Darcy said, "Yes, I know. We will all be thrown out into the hedgerows." Rolling his eyes, he added emphasis to how ludicrous he thought the idea was.

"No, Lizzy. Really think about what will happen if Papa dies. We have no money to speak of, no relations who have room - much less the money - to put us up, and no appreciable skills or prospects. We really would be left penniless with nowhere to go. Not that you should be the one to have to save us but that is where Mama is coming from."

For the first time, Darcy thought about the very real problems the Bennet ladies would face if they did not succeed in marrying comfortably. In his mind Mrs. Bennet was far too pushy with her daughters, shoving them in the direction of any eligible bachelor, however perhaps her motives were not as purely mercenary as he had once thought them to be. In all likelihood, she really did care about their happiness, somewhere deep down inside.

"You are correct, as usual, dear Jane. Perhaps I have been too hard on Mama. But that does not mean that I will rethink my refusal of Mr. Collins."

Jane laughed quietly on her way out of the room and said, "I should hope not! I will see you at dinner, Lizzy. I am going to go work in the garden. It looks like we may have a freeze so I want to cover some of the last flowers."

Chapter 10: Elizabeth

Upon returning to Netherfield, Elizabeth was almost immediately accosted by Miss Bingley. Well, perhaps 'accosted' is a bit strong. 'Sought out' might be more accurate. Apparently, Miss Bingley wanted to get Darcy's opinion. Placing her hand on Mr. Darcy's arm, Miss Bingley began to explain the issue. She felt it was necessary to redecorate but Charles did not. If she was expected to act as hostess, the 'hideous papers' in the public rooms (which Elizabeth quite liked) would need to be replaced. Not being in the mood to deal with Caroline's fawning over Mr. Darcy, Elizabeth bade her forgiveness instead.

"Forgive me, Miss Bingley, but this discussion will have to wait. I find I am in dreadful need of a change of clothes after such a long ride." Then she turned to the nearest footman, "Samuel, please have a hot bath prepared," and headed up the stairs without a backward glance for Miss Bingley. Miss Bingley, of course, stood for a moment shocked, and then insulted.

Once in Darcy's room, Elizabeth relaxed. Being around Caroline Bingley always put her on edge for she had clearly set her cap at Mr. Darcy. Though Elizabeth was sure many women had, it bothered her that Caroline seemed to think she was entitled to be the next Mistress of Pemberley. Her mien was so haughty, like she was better than everyone else. Elizabeth was not even sure that Caroline held affection for Mr. Darcy, only that she coveted his position in society and his wealth.

Elizabeth found she was excessively relieved that Mr. Darcy did not hold any affection for the woman. Not only so she would not be put in an awkward position but also because she discovered herself to be strangely protective of Mr. Darcy due to the reversal of their circumstances. She believed, or rather hoped, Mr. Darcy felt the same.

She began to undress and ready herself for the bath when she caught sight of her reflection, or rather *his* reflection in the mirror which stood in the corner of the room. Though still in breeches from earlier, she had removed his shirt and the sight of a shirtless Mr. Darcy had at first startled and then fascinated her. She stepped toward the lovely, cheval mirror and simply stared at him. He was surprisingly lean and muscular for a gentleman which suggested he was not a stranger to physical labor. Somehow, she was not wholly shocked by the idea that he might take a more active role in his estate than she once would have believed.

Without thinking she raised her, rather *his,* hand and ran it along his chest. It was so different. Where she was soft, he was hard and he had a light cover of hair that ran down the center of his stomach. Before she knew it her breathing changed and she felt a change in his body… down there. 'Oh dear, have I done something wrong?' She slowly unfastened his breeches to assess the problem. 'Oh heavens, it looks quite swollen. I don't recall injuring myself. No, this only just occurred.'

She decided to 'inspect' *it* for any signs of what may have caused it to be in this state. What she found was not what she expected. Her very touch appeared to increase the swelling and was quite pleasurable. Just then she caught sight of the mirror again which pulled her out of her haze and she quickly moved away to the bath.

Stepping in, Elizabeth shivered. 'I guess I stood there longer than I realized as the water is now quite cold.' The cold water also quickly took care of the other problem she had, "Oh thank goodness," she sighed. While not completely sure, she felt as if she had unintentionally crossed a boundary. Would Mr. Darcy be angry or embarrassed? She had not meant for anything untoward to occur. Had it?

****

"There you are, Darcy!" Bingley called as she walked by the study doors. Elizabeth stopped and seeing only Bingley in there, decided to enter. Walking over to the brandy cart, she poured herself a small glass - hoping that is what Mr. Darcy would have done. "What can I do for you, Charles?"

Here Bingley became very concerned. "Are you alright, Darce? You never drink early in the day, or much at all come to think of it."

Drat. I am trying too hard to manly. "I am quite well. I had an excellent ride with Hector this morning and now I thought to look in on you. What plans have you for the day?"

Not completely convinced, and yet not one to challenge his dear friend, Bingley let the matter drop. "Well, we have been invited to the Lucus' party tonight. I hear the lovely Bennet ladies will be there." That last bit he added with some enthusiasm.

Smiling, Elizabeth teased, "Is there a particular Bennet lady you wish to see?"

"Miss Jane Bennet, of course! How could you even question?" Then it dawned on him that Darcy was teasing him. "You jest! See Darce, I knew you hit your head harder the other day than you cared to admit. First you drink in the middle of the day, now you *jest*! Shall I call your physician from London?" Bingley made this speech only half-jokingly; he had noticed Darcy was acting a little out of character. Nothing outlandish, just different.

"First of all, I have had one, SMALL drink and I simply find I am in a good mood so that accounts for my teasing just now. Would you prefer I go back to brooding as I have been wont to do of late?" Here Elizabeth hoped she was right; perhaps Darcy had not been brooding except when in public. Mayhap, he was more lighthearted when it was just he and Mr. Bingley.

"No, no. I am glad to see you rising out of the darkness that consumed you this summer. You take on far too much yourself, man. I sometimes worry it has aged you beyond your 28 years."

28 years old? I had no idea. At times, he looks much older, 35 even. Other times, like when he smiles (which she had only seen him do once and it had utterly transformed him), he looked to be only in his early 20s. What weight he must shoulder to be always so stoic?

While she had been lost in thought, Bingley had been rambling happily about tonight and the chance to see 'his angel' again. Rejoining the conversation, she asked, "Will your sisters and Hurst be attending with us?"

"Louisa is still feeling under the weather and though Hurst loves a good card game, he has opted to stay with her. Caroline will be coming, of course. I think she wants to keep you away from Miss Elizabeth and her 'fine eyes'."

Upon seeing the look of confusion on Darcy's face, added, "Don't act as if you have forgotten admitting that you think Miss Elizabeth has fine eyes or that you think her complexion is often brightened by her walking! You're fooling no one, my old friend."

As Bingley laughed, Elizabeth joined in so as not to seem odd but on the inside her stomach was once again feeling that nervous tingling sensation that she felt earlier today while riding with Darcy. Did he, in fact, think she was pretty? What of his comment at the assembly? Clearly he had changed his opinion at some point but to what degree? And why should it matter?

They spoke for a while longer before she excused herself saying she had some letters to write before they left. With that,

Elizabeth made her way to the library for some solitary reflection.

Mr. Darcy had said to read his letter in his room but she still felt a little embarrassed from earlier. So she settled into a large wingback chair in front of the fire. So engrossed was she in the scandalous contents of the letter (Mr. Wickham attempting to elope with Mr. Darcy's 15 year old sister) that she did not realize Miss Bingley and Mrs. Hurst had entered the library until the two ladies were in the middle of what was clearly a very private conversation. Neither had seen Mr. Darcy sitting by the fire as he was facing away from them.

Mrs. Hurst spoke softly at first as if breaking bad news to a child. "Caroline, Mr. Hurst and I are expecting."

"Expecting what, Louisa? Oh! *Expecting!* Well, I suppose congratulations are in order." Less than enthusiastic, Miss Bingley feigned interest, "When is this blessed event to occur?"

"Early spring. I believe I am in the third month. But Caroline, with a child coming we will be curtailing much of our travel and entertaining. At least, for a while. You may find living with us, well, rather boring."

"Yes, well. I don't plan to be single much longer. Mr. Darcy is going to declare himself soon. This time, I am sure of it. Now that he has seen the wretched society the country has to offer (and clearly there is no one in Derbyshire or he would have already been attached), he cannot help but see the benefits that our union will bring."

Before Louisa could contradict her, Caroline continued, "I am the sister of his dearest friend; I am one of the most accomplished women of his acquaintance; he was very impressed with how well the ball last week turned out and that was a simple country affair. There really is no logical reason he shouldn't desire me to be the Mistress of Pemberley."

Hoping for a gentle tone Louisa proceeded with caution, "Logic is not the only issue at play. Have you not noticed that Mr. Darcy has lately paid marked attention to Miss Elizabeth Bennet?"

"Really Louisa! I am surprised at you! Eliza Bennet is a novelty at best. She is impertinent, uncouth, and altogether unsuitable for a man of Mr. Darcy's quality and station!" The thought that even *Louisa* had begun to lose faith stung. No matter, Caroline Bingley was not one to be deterred from what she had set her mind to.

Louisa, fairly certain that Caroline was fighting a losing battle, decided to change tactics. "It has been over 5 years, Caroline. Do you not think that you ought to at least *consider* the possibility that Mr. Darcy might *not* declare himself? What if he truly has feelings for Miss Elizabeth? You are unlikely to sway him then."

"He wouldn't be so foolish as to align himself with such a family. Her father may be a 'gentleman' but the family is hardly worth notice. However, if Mr. Darcy chooses to think with, ahem, appendages other than his head, well… perhaps he will need to be nudged along."

Just then, when Elizabeth was unsure if she could hold her tongue a moment longer, Mr. Hurst entered the library looking for his wife and effectively halting the conversation.

"Louisa, dear," he said as he offered her his arm, "you must rest. You are in a delicate way. Come now and take a nap. I shall wake you when it is time for dinner."

Elizabeth thought she had never heard his voice so tender before. Perhaps Mr. Hurst drank as often as he did to escape from his conniving sister-in-law. Much more time spent in her presence and Elizabeth thought she might well imbibe a few herself.

The happy couple left the library arm in arm, leaving Miss Bingley to her own devices. Fortunately for Elizabeth, Caroline - despite her attempts to appear otherwise - held no affection for reading and so, left the library in search of another diversion.

'Maybe I will come across Mr. Darcy,' Caroline thought with a troublesome gleam in her eye. It was then that she began to hatch a plan for *finally* catching Mr. Darcy. 'He may try to delay the inevitable, but I am done playing games.' Caroline was not a quitter and she was not used to losing. No, Mr. Darcy would declare himself to her one way or another, and soon.

Chapter 11: Darcy

Darcy took particular care in dressing Elizabeth for the dinner party because, honestly, he delighted in helping Elizabeth appear to her greatest advantage. Her dark, emerald eyes would be accentuated by this blue-green evening gown with delicate pearl beading. He even asked Jane to help put pearls in her hair as well.

While Jane did not question Elizabeth about her careful preparations, she did note that Elizabeth had been taking special care to look nice when she knew she would be in the presence of the party from Netherfield and attributed this to wanting Mr. Darcy's approval. However, Jane was not sure that Lizzy was ready to admit her feelings to anyone - or even if she had admitted them to herself - so she held her tongue.

Descending the staircase, the elder sisters and Mr. Collins (who still held the unreasonable hope of winning Elizabeth's hand) donned their cloaks and gloves in preparation for departure. Punctual by nature, it did not take long for Mr. Darcy to become impatient waiting for Kitty, Lydia, and Mrs. Bennet to join them. After waiting a full 15 minutes, Darcy looked at Mr.

Bennet and, knowing Elizabeth was her father's favorite, asked, "Papa? Is it not ridiculous that the whole family is made late because Kitty and Lydia cannot figure out who gets which ribbons? Can we not leave and send the carriage back to fetch them after? Then maybe next time, they would be more considerate of others."

Seeing an opportunity to have some time in the company of the ladies, Mr. Collins quickly offered his assistance. "Yes, I could easily take those who are ready and send the carriage back for you and the others, Sir."

Mr. Bennet, who did not like Mr. Collins anyway, could not agree to allowing his daughters out without a parental chaperone (not that he usually cared but he didn't appreciate the way Collins openly and indelicately stared at Elizabeth). "I would be delighted to accept your offer with one modification: *I* will go in the first carriage and *you* will stay with the ladies until they are prepared. Thank you, Sir."

Darcy chuckled to himself for he immediately saw what Mr. Bennet was about. It may be that the old-goat was not as lackadaisical as he had thought him to be. Since having imparted the information regarding Wickham's true character, Mr. Bennet seemed determined to protect his rather vulnerable family. This was a side of Mr. Bennet that Darcy could respect.

Upon arriving at Lucas Lodge, Darcy followed Jane's lead as she sought out their good friend, Charlotte Lucas.

"Good evening Jane, Lizzy. Where have you hidden your mother and sisters?" Darcy knew that, next to Jane, Charlotte was Elizabeth's closest friend so he determined that no offense was meant in her remark. This was confirmed when Jane answered Charlotte with a small chuckle.

"Well, as usual, there we all were: Papa, Lizzy, Mary, Mr. Collins, and myself waiting - once again - on Kitty, Lydia, and Mama. Then Lizzy spoke up saying that she doesn't think we should all suffer because they can't get ready on time."

Here Darcy interrupted, adding with his own chuckle, "Come now, Jane, I do believe my argument was a bit more eloquent than that. You make me sound like a petulant teenager."

Jane happily continued, "Of course, my apologies. So after some discussion about carriage arrangements, Papa decided to escort us first and send the carriage back for them. It was the most pleasant ride we have had in some time!"

Feigning shock Charlotte chided, "Jane Bennet! That is the closest thing to an unkind word as I have heard from you! Tsk, Tsk." At this, all three burst into laughter. They may have garnered more attention from others had it not been for the arrival of both the Netherfield party and the remaining Bennets, simultaneously.

As the doors opened to admit the guests to the parlor, Lydia dragged Kitty into the room exclaiming that "thank goodness we have finally arrived. Sorry to have been so late but we had to *wait* for the carriage to return!" She continued, complaining to no one in particular that had it not been for Mr. Collins and her father joining the party they could have all fit into one, and on and on, lamenting that she had missed even a moment of the evening's entertainment.

Mrs. Bennet was not much better telling Lady Lucas that she did not know why *she* had been left out of the first trip. It was not as if anyone would have missed her husband's or even Mary's company for a short while. Jane colored at this exclamation and looked apologetically to Charlotte.

Darcy noted to the credit of every one of the guests present - with the exception of Caroline Bingley - no one rolled their eyes or whispered behind their fans. They seemed to take it in stride, continuing with their conversations. Miss Bingley of course, turned to Elizabeth, whom she of course thought was Darcy, whispered something, and laughed. Elizabeth colored and said nothing. Darcy immediately felt ashamed that he had in the past allowed Miss Bingley to behave this way and therefore make him guilty by association. It was no wonder Elizabeth thought so meanly of him. He had, by not curbing Caroline's catty remarks, essentially condoned them. Elizabeth looked up and met Darcy's eyes. They each seemed to apologize to the other. However, they could not speak just now so actual apologies would have to wait. At present, he would have to be content to continue his talk with Jane and Charlotte, both of whom he found to be much more interesting than many ladies of his acquaintance.

Elizabeth and Bingley, together, walked toward Mr. Bennet and began a rather lively discussion of the 'conflict' on the continent. Elizabeth realized that she had been missing this level of debate since this situation with Darcy had occurred. No one in the Netherfield party enjoyed a good debate. While Bingley was knowledgeable, he was not generally comfortable arguing his point. Even tonight he had mostly asked questions or agreed with one man's point or another's.

Elizabeth relished the opportunity to stretch her mind. She and Mr. Bennet often played Devil's Advocate when discussing current events. At several points throughout the conversation, Mr. Bennet looked at her and shook his head. "You know Sir, my daughter Elizabeth said something very similar just the other day. It seems the two of you have much in common." Each time, Elizabeth would force herself to take moment to consider if she was staying in character or misrepresenting how Darcy might feel upon the matter.

Shortly before dinner was called the younger men excused themselves to 'make the rounds' ensuring that they found the company of the Miss Bennets in time to escort them in for dinner. As they approached, Charlotte made an excuse about needing to speak to her mother and conveniently extricated herself from the conversation. Almost immediately following her departure, dinner was announced and each gentleman took his preferred lady's arm to lead them into the dining room.

Dinner was a sumptuous affair but it was not so formal as to make the atmosphere stiff. Everyone seemed happy with their dinner partners, save Caroline Bingley who was seated between Mr. Henry Lucas on the left and Mr. Collins on the right. While Henry was a nice young man, he was not rich enough to warrant her notice. Caroline spoke just enough to each to not insult her hosts.

In between courses, when everyone seemed sufficiently engrossed in their own conversations, Elizabeth took the opportunity to pass Darcy a note under the table. He was quite surprised that Elizabeth would take such a risk. For a gentleman seen giving a lady a letter would face serious consequences. Whatever the contents, Darcy knew it must be of utmost import. He took it quickly and placed it in the pocket of his dress (he made sure to only wear dresses *with* pockets if he would not have a reticule, for he was still quite embarrassed).

"Looking down to indicate the letter she had passed him, Elizabeth quietly said, "I heard something most interesting today that I thought you might like to know." Looking around to make sure she was not overheard, she whispered, "Miss Bingley."

"Oh," he whispered in return. Then raising his voice back to its normal level, asked, "And how are you enjoying your stay at Netherfield, Sir? Have you seen much of the countryside?" Darcy asked her, knowing full well Elizabeth would have many positive things to say.

"I have Miss Elizabeth. But I am sure there is still much left to see. I rode this morning for some time and enjoyed myself immensely." Here she let a grin play across her features, "I plan to go out again tomorrow and see what other wonders there are to behold. I have heard tales of a small lake and wondered if it is suitable for fishing."

Fortunately for Mr. Darcy, who truly had no idea how to answer, Mr. Bennet chimed in. "I believe, Mr. Darcy, that the lake you speak of has not been stocked for some time. If you find it lacking, you gentlemen may certainly come to Longbourn and fish in ours. With 5 daughters, it doesn't get the use it should, though it is stocked annually. In fact, it has been too long since I have been out there myself! "

Elizabeth was dumbstruck. This was the first time in her memory her father had invited company to his home of his own volition. He must think highly of Mr. Darcy to have opened his home and even offered to join him! She and Bingley answered the invitation in unison, "Thank you, Sir!" Elizabeth adding, "We'd like that very much; that's very generous of you."

After dinner the ladies excused themselves to the parlor while the gentlemen enjoyed a drink or two. Elizabeth was very excited and curious to take part in the ritual separation of the sexes. She would never - as a lady - have been privy to this side. Once all the ladies were gone, the men began to talk across the table so that all could take part. It was rather informal which did not surprise her. The topics of conversation ranged from politics to the very gossip she would have expected to hear while amongst the ladies. She would have been shocked if she did not find it so amusing to hear these men, who regularly eschewed such talk while in mixed company, take part as eagerly as the butcher's and baker's wives.

"So Henry? How much longer before you ask Annabelle to marry you? You've been sweethearts since you were nine!" Mr. Bennet teased congenially. Everyone knew that Henry and Annie had been made for one another and that they would more than likely get married this summer after he finished school.

"Actually, I plan to ask her on New Year's Eve at midnight!" Henry was so excited but swore them all to secrecy. "I want it to be a surprise."

Oh my, who would have thought that this what men speak of while we women are in the parlor speaking of the same things? Elizabeth was amazed. And then, the discussion turned more personal. Her father - less than delicately - suggested that he hoped any of his daughters' suitors would not make them wait so long. He shared a look with Sir William who then - not so subtly - looked at Bingley. *Ugh, while Father is not as bad as Mama, he is not far off. How embarrassing*, she thought to herself.

Bingley coughed nervously. Elizabeth knew that he had growing affection for Jane and even believed him to be close to a declaration but… Her musings were interrupted by Bingley's next, most unexpected statement.

"Actually, Mr. Bennet, I was hoping to speak with you privately on the morrow." Bingley continued, nervous but determined.

At once everyone in the room let out a cheer.

Sir William congratulated, "Bravo, my boy! Jane is quite a lady!"

Mr. Collins offered his services for the big day.

Mr. Bennet just smiled and said, "'Bout time my boy! I will be available all morning."

Elizabeth was so moved, she almost forgot that Darcy would be expected to offer congratulations as well. "Charles, I offer you my sincerest congratulations. You and Miss Bennet are well suited; I'm sure you will both be very happy."

As she sat there, Elizabeth realized it would not be long before she lost her dearest sister, Jane. She only hoped that she would not spend her last days as Jane's sister trapped in Darcy's body and living at Netherfield.

Meanwhile, in the parlor amongst the ladies, Darcy found himself quite out of his depth. Once again he'd joined Jane and Charlotte and the topic of discussion quickly turned to Mr. Bingley. Charlotte began by turning to Jane, "Well, it is quite obvious to me that Mr. Bingley is smitten with you. However, if I were not as well acquainted with you as I am, I would not be able to say for certain whether or not you returned his feelings."

Jane seemed quite taken aback. "But I do!" Turning to Elizabeth she questioned with growing panic, "You can tell, can't you Lizzy? I mean, I don't want to wear my heart on my sleeve for fear of gossip but I want Mr. Bingley to be able to discern my feelings. You do think *he* understands, do you not?"

Darcy, seeing the affection for his friend that he hoped to one day be the recipient of from Elizabeth answered her gently, "Yes, dear. I am sure that unless your Mr. Bingley is a fool, he can discern your feelings."

Jane let out a small, unsure laugh. "He is not *my* Mr. Bingley, Lizzy."

"Perhaps, not yet. But I cannot imagine it will be long."

They were unable to continue because Miss Bingley joined them. "Miss Lucas, Jane, Eliza. It's been a lovely evening so far has it not? I do not usually enjoy such informal dinner parties but tonight has been positively... quaint." She said this in a pleasant manner but the underlying message was quite clear: 'Your poor, country gatherings are far below my usual entertainment, but it is better than nothing.'

"Thank you, Miss Bingley, we are so glad you could join us. I'm sure you're used to much larger affairs in London as I am sure your father had to entertain his business associates regularly. But we do the best we can in our little corner of the country."

Darcy had to cough to stifle a laugh. *Bravo, Miss Lucas. Don't let Caroline belittle you in your own home.* Darcy should not have been surprised that Elizabeth's closest friend would be clever but he had thought Charlotte was more mild-mannered than that. Tonight, he was heartily pleased to see she was not.

The rest of the evening was spent pleasantly conversing with various guests. Upon the arrival of the gentlemen, Jane and Bingley quickly found their way to the fireplace where they could speak in relative privacy. And while Darcy wanted to speak with Elizabeth (he could hardly wait to read the letter she had given him), every time he drew near to Elizabeth, Caroline seemed to appear at Elizabeth's side. He smiled to himself. '*Of course*,' he thought, '*Caroline would do anything to keep Elizabeth away from me and right now she thinks Elizabeth is me. Poor Elizabeth must be miserable*'.

When he had begun to lose hope of having another chance to speak to her before the night was over, he saw Elizabeth step out onto the terrace alone. Apparently Miss Bingley had drawn into conversation with Lady Lucas and Elizabeth had used this opportunity to escape.

Darcy waited a moment and then followed her, careful to not be seen. The night sky was beautiful. As if she sensed his presence, Elizabeth said, "This reminds me of the night sky during the Netherfield Ball. It was so clear and bright. I wished upon a star, that night.' She laughed a quiet, unsure laugh, "I know, you probably think that's childish."

Stepping up to the railing but far enough to maintain propriety. "Not at all, as I recall, I too wished on a star that evening."

"Wait, you did too? And then we woke up switched the next morning! Don't you see, that must be what happened? What did you wish for?"

He looked uncomfortable, "Understanding." He said it simply enough but it seemed the word was packed with a deeper meaning.

She thought for a moment. "Me too, in a way. Maybe we just need to wish ourselves back!" Then she turned to look up at the sky, searching for a shooting star. But inexplicably, where thousands of stars had been visible just a moment ago, now only dark clouds remained.

Hope faded from Elizabeth's face. Wanting to bring her comfort, Darcy took her hand, "Perhaps we are not ready. Perhaps we have not learned what we need to learn. I am convinced this is not just a cosmic joke. There is a reason we have been placed in this situation, Miss Elizabeth. We will figure this out."

"At least now we know *how* the switch occurred." Then she squeezed his hand and let go. "We should go back inside. Those clouds promise rain."

Chapter 12: Darcy

As soon as Darcy arrived back at Longbourn, he headed upstairs to bed citing 'a dreadful headache'. Jane gave him a concerned look, but he assured her a good night's sleep was all the cure he'd need. Once safely alone in Elizabeth's room, Darcy took out the letter Elizabeth had given him at dinner.

Mr. Darcy,

I know it is improper to write to you but it could not be helped. This afternoon, I was in the library when Mrs. Hurst and Miss Bingley entered. They must not have seen me however, as their conversation was of a most personal nature.

You may be pleased to learn that Mrs. Hurst is expecting and while it is not yet general knowledge - I am not even sure Mr. Bingley knows - she will not be able to hide it much longer. It explains her frequent bouts of illness and near constant fatigue. Mr. Hurst has been most attentive. Really, it has been heartwarming to watch.

The rest of the conversation however, took a rather disturbing turn. Mrs. Hurst was attempting to make Miss Bingley see reason with regard to her hopes of 'catching' you. For this I must give Mrs. Hurst credit. Nevertheless, Miss Bingley insisted that you were likely to declare yourself to her soon especially after seeing what little the country has to offer - and here I must say I felt a personal affront - by way of suitable women. I do not mean to imply that I am a suitable choice rather that the country is not devoid of suitable ladies. Many of whom I cannot think you would find lacking.

I digress, the crux of the matter came toward the end of the conversation when Miss Bingley alluded to the fact that "Perhaps he needs to be nudged along". I can only conclude that she means to force your hand in some way. Would she go so far as to compromise you?

I asked Davies to sleep in your dressing room out of caution. And do you know his response? He said, he had already been doing so for some time as he had sensed Miss Bingley growing desperate in recent weeks. Then he seemed almost embarrassed for having been so bold.

I thanked him for his loyalty and assured him that, in the future, he should always feel comfortable bringing these concerns to my attention. I hope I have not overstepped but he was so sincere.

Of course, I will also be on my guard to safeguard your reputation.

Sincerely,
E. B.

P.S. I hope you are finding your way in a woman's world. I must admit, it makes me smile just a bit to know that while your world is different from mine, it cannot possibly be as foreign as being in a house full of women must be to you.

Darcy put the letter on the bed and began to undress. His thoughts were far from coherent and jumped from one to another. Of course he had known of Miss Bingley's intentions for some time but even he was surprised by this development. And, *of course*, Elizabeth would not consider herself as the most suitable candidate for Mistress of Pemberley when he had begun to consider her the *only* candidate. How long had Davies been sleeping in his dressing room? He would have to raise his pay. He had always liked and trusted the man, but now he knew he owed him more that he had realized.

One by one, he removed the pins from Elizabeth's long, thick curls. He ran his fingers through them and pulled a curl to his face, deeply inhaling her scent - lavender and rose water. If he closed his eyes he could imagine he was himself again with his face buried in those curls. But he wouldn't close his eyes because if he did, he would take these imaginings too far.

His dreams, though, he could not control and he found that every night he explored those soft curves that tortured him so during daylight hours. He always started with her hair. It had tempted him since he first saw her. But then he moved to her heavenly lips, her cheeks, her long, soft neck, and on down removing her night shift so he had unfettered access to the swells of her full breasts. He cupped them in his hands, trailing kisses over them until he reached... well he need not dwell on his dreams for they only made him yearn for her more.

It was always near this point in this most satisfying dream that he would awake, covered in sweat and breathing deeply. He noted that unlike similar dreams before this switch occurred, Elizabeth's body had reacted very differently. Darcy felt somewhat ashamed at not being able to control his desires and therefore invading this part of Elizabeth's privacy. But he knew there was little he could do about it. The only difference between his dreams now and the ones he had before was that now he knew what she looked and felt like and it made them all the more torturous.

*****

The next morning was cold and wet. Darcy had wanted to go out walking but he was not sure even Elizabeth would have gone out today. He dressed and made his way downstairs to eat. At some point today Bingley would be coming by. A little rain was unlikely to deter him from the meeting Elizabeth had informed Darcy was set for today.

Darcy was proud of his friend. It was clear that he had strong feelings for Jane, just like it was clear that Bingley's sisters strongly opposed the match. It was not so long ago that Charles might have been swayed by their opinion (or even Darcy's) but he had rented Netherfield despite their lamenting the distance from London (and additionally, Caroline's lamenting the distance from Pemberley). Darcy had to admit that Bingley still at times relied too much on his advice and, to that end, he was glad that this switch had removed the situation from his influence as he would likely have advised against the match. But the last few days at Longbourn had changed his opinion on so many things. He was now very much in favor of it.

One and two at a time, the rest of the ladies joined him in the parlor as there was little else to do on a rainy day. Darcy sat with a book to avoid having to engage in too much conversation, especially with Mrs. Bennet or the two youngest sisters. He found he enjoyed Jane's company and that even Mary could be amusing, although Darcy was not altogether sure she meant to be. Mr. Collins was still far too attentive and Darcy was increasingly uncomfortable by his rather less than subtle overtures and his constant staring. 'Is this how Elizabeth felt when I 'stared'?" For he was quite certain from all that Jane said that he had. Although, he was equally certain that - though tempting - he never stared openly at her bosom as Mr. Collins did. If that didn't stop, Darcy would have to put a stop to it in a less than polite manner. Though he did not have his usual strength to aid him, he knew how to make his point clear to the gentleman.

"Lizzy? You haven't turned a page in almost half an hour. Are you well?" Mary asked with genuine concern.

"I'm sorry. I wasn't able to walk out this morning and I fear I am bit out of sorts."

"La Lizzy, you have been acting odd since the ball at Netherfield! Are you still upset that Wickham wasn't there?"

"Thank you, Lydia. Your concern is endearing," Darcy answered sarcastically. And as usual, neither Lydia nor Mrs. Bennet caught on. However, Darcy did notice Kitty stifling a small chuckle. There might be hope for her yet. In a more serious tone, he added, "And, no. You know what Papa said: Mr. Wickham is not to be trusted,"

Returning to the topic of exercise, Mr. Collins felt it prudent to add his opinion, "In your sex, manly exercises are never graceful. A tone and figure of the masculine kind are always forbidding. Men of sensibility desire in every woman soft features a form not robust and demeanor delicate and gentle Nature appears to have formed the (mental) faculties of your sex…" Mr. Collins liked to quote Fordyce whenever he could. And Mary often added her assent.

However, perhaps today it would have been wiser for Mr. Collins to have remained silent. For Darcy had no doubt that he was the better educated of the two, even if it weren't for the fact that he considered all Mr. Collins' philosophies on life to be old fashioned and outdated.

Half to himself, Darcy replied aloud, "Taught from their infancy that beauty is woman's sceptre, the mind shapes itself to the body, and, roaming round its gilt cage, only seeks to adorn its prison."

Mr. Collins looked aghast! "Cousin Elizabeth, did you just quote that heretic Mary Wollstonecraft? I hardly think that is suitable material for a gentlewoman. If we are to wed, Wollstonecraft will have no part in our household!"

"Then it is fortunate that we are not to wed, as I have already explained!" With that, Darcy got up from his seat and made his way out to the garden. It may be a little damp still but at least it was quiet. Before he was fully out of the room, Darcy looked back to see Mary and Mr. Collins speaking quietly to one another sporting equally disapproving scowls, Mrs. Bennet looked fit to be tied, and Jane looked concerned. She feared that if Elizabeth was not careful, she may find herself in the middle of a war between their Mother and Father. If that became the case, Jane was not sure how long their Father would fight for Elizabeth.

That is when it came to him… Mr. Collins would be happier with Mary! How he had not seen it before was beyond him.

But, now that he had, Darcy would do all he could to steer Mr. Collins in that direction.

However alike they were, Mr. Darcy could foresee one, rather large, hurdle: Mary was plain; not altogether unattractive but she did absolutely *nothing* to put herself to an advantage. Darcy began to formulate a plan.

Chapter 13: Darcy

Darcy was pretty pleased with himself. Not only would his plan rescue Elizabeth from the clutches of the ridiculous Mr. Collins, but it would also bestow - what he could only view as - a kindness upon Mary, whom he viewed as the often overlooked Bennet sister. Re-entering the parlor, Darcy managed to make eye contact with Jane and silently urged her to join him at the window seat.

"Have you quite recovered from your earlier temper, Lizzy? Not that it was unwarranted, but you know Mama will have some choice words for you later."

"That is what I wanted to talk to you about, Jane. I have a plan. A rather brilliant one, if I do say so, but I will need your help. Have you not noticed how well suited Mr. Collins and Mary are for one another? I know, you will say she is young but, really, she is 19 and I think they would do well together. They think so alike. I believe that the only obstacle in their path is that Mr. Collins sees her as 'the plain sister.' If we could convince Mama that Mary would be the better choice, do you think mama would allow us to make Mary over?"

Looking at Lizzy with more than a little concern, Jane questioned, "Make her over, how? She is lovely as she is."

This may be harder than he thought if Jane didn't even like the idea. "*I* know she is and *you* know she is but Mr. Collins is a man and sometimes they need help seeing inner beauty. I don't want to change who Mary is… I just want to *accentuate* her positive qualities."

Smiling, "When did you become such an expert on men, Lizzy?" Adding after a short pause, "I love the idea. It is high time someone made Mary feel as special as she is."

"I agree. But, Jane, I think you should speak to Mama about it tonight before dinner. Mama always listens to you more than me. And that way, she can help us plan how to get Mary to agree to go shopping with us." With that, Darcy and Jane set about making plans for what needed to be done. New ribbons to retrim her dresses and perhaps even a new bonnet would need to be purchased. Mary's bonnets were the oldest of any of the sisters so their need of being replaced was unlikely to be questioned. Jane even thought to include Kitty in their plans as she really had a talent for picking flattering colors and cuts for ribbons and bonnets. Even Lydia tended to ask Kitty's opinion, though she always pretended that her opinion had been just the same.

Later that afternoon, with Mary practicing the piano forte in the front room, Mr. Collins writing yet another letter to Lady Catherine, and Mrs. Bennet and Lydia each napping, the three ladies (Jane, Lizzy, and Kitty) met in the parlor to plan the next steps. They debated asking Lydia to join in and had almost decided against it, fearing that her over exuberance would make Mary hesitant to take part at all, when Kitty pointed out that Mama would not stand for the others to have a secret that her favorite was not a party to. So Kitty was dispatched to quietly retrieve Lydia. The latter was none too happy until she realized why she had been woken up and quickly her annoyance turned to excitement. For even Lydia needed a fresh diversion now and again.

There was one detail they had not yet worked out: how to get Mary to allow herself to be made over. Surprisingly, it was Lydia who pointed out the obvious, "La, you lot are so thick! Mary is desperate for Mr. Collins' approval - though I can't see why; he is so…"

"Lydia!" Darcy interrupted, "Your point?"

"Oh yes, well, she is half in love with him already. I think she will do almost anything to get his attention… within the bounds of propriety. You know how she is about 'a proper lady' this and 'a proper lady' that."

They looked at each other, dumbstruck that Lydia may have a valid point. Darcy spoke up, "Okay, we will simply offer to help her accentuate her positive qualities."

"Ooooh, this will be so much fun! When do we start?" Kitty bounced up and down on the settee. Now all that was left was convincing Mrs. Bennet and Mary.

*****

Shortly before dinner, when everyone else was distracted (or appeared to be), Jane approached Mrs. Bennet. "Mama, may I speak with you for a moment… privately?"

"Of course, Janey. Is something troubling you? Have you quarreled with Mr. Bingley?" Panic began to suffuse Mrs. Bennet's face.

"No, Mama. I wanted to talk to you about Mr. Collins."

"Oh. I know, this business with Lizzy rejecting the poor man is trying my poor nerves! What can she be thinking?"

"I believe I have an alternative that may make everyone truly happy," adding, "and secure Longbourn," to appeal to her mother.

Jane explained the plan to Mrs. Bennet, who was skeptical at first but after some thought, decided that perhaps Lizzy didn't deserve Mr. Collins and Longbourn. "Well, I suppose that Mary could be acceptable. But Mr. Collins has his eye on Lizzy, ungrateful, headstrong girl."

"Mama, if you agree, my sisters and I would like to help Mary gain his attention by making her over. Some new ribbons on her dresses, a new bonnet, and some help dressing her hair would go a long way toward making her less plain. In fact, I think she only appears plain due to her lack of effort in that area."

"Hmm, you may be right Jane. It would do me proud to see Mary dressed up for once. None of *my* girls should ever be looked down upon! But Lizzy is not off the hook, if this plan does not work, I will expect her to do her duty by this family!"

Knowing Lizzy was not likely to agree but needing their mother's help, Jane simply replied, "Of course, Mama. Thank you." Then she left the room before Mrs. Bennet could change her mind.

*****

Dinner was the usual chaotic event. They had planned for Kitty to ask for permission to walk to Meryton the next day to buy some ribbons. Then Lydia would, characteristically, show her enthusiasm for the plan. Jane and Darcy would agree to chaperone the younger girls as long as Mary agreed to come as well since at one point Jane and Lizzy needed to stop by the modiste to pick up some 'essentials'. As expected Mr. Collins colored at the implication that the ladies needed to buy intimate items, effectively preventing him from attempting to join the party. Mr. Bennet looked across the table at his daughters, sure they were up to something but not curious enough to inquire as to what. Time would tell.

However, as the plan began to unfold, Mrs. Bennet spoke up, "Actually girls, I think we all need a trip to the modiste. Every one of you could stand to update to your 'essentials' and perhaps we can peruse some other baubles while we are out."

Kitty and Lydia immediately squealed with excitement, Mary shrugged as it appeared she had no choice and she did not object to well-fitting undergarments as all young ladies needed them, while Jane and Elizabeth sat in stunned silence. It was rare for Mrs. Bennet to join the girls shopping but not altogether unwelcome. In fact, it may be quite helpful to have her there to make additional purchases as Mary would not likely protest her mother's decisions - unless they included excess ruffles. Mary would not stand for ruffles. All in all, tomorrow was shaping up to be an interesting day.

Mr. Bennet sat at the table uncharacteristically quiet. This day had been an eventful one for him as well. Earlier in the day, unbeknownst to the rest of the family, he had indeed had a meeting with Mr. Bingley. Bingley had, of course, come to ask permission to court Miss Bennet. While Mr. Bennet had every intention of saying yes, he did not feel he would be doing his job as a father if he did not let the young man sweat a little. Mr. Bingley had good prospects and a respectable family and Mr. Bennet knew he'd be a fool not to give his blessing. But if he were honest, he knew that no matter how much he may like Mr. Bingley, if he'd been asking to court his Lizzy, he was not sure he would approve. Lizzy needed someone more… intellectual? Clever? Just more; more challenging. Lizzy would not be happy with an amiable sort like Bingley. She'd get bored. And that was one of the things he loved best about her… she needed to be challenged. He despaired that someday she would find such a man for then he would lose her. He looked over at Darcy, seeing his beloved Lizzy and thinking of losing her made his heart ache.

Chapter 14: Elizabeth

The next morning, earlier than was perhaps strictly proper, Mr. Bingley and Mr. Darcy came to call. All the ladies of the house flew into a frenzy freshening up the parlor to receive guests and Darcy silently wondered if this happened every time he and Bingley had come to visit in the past. Hill announced the guests and Mr. Bingley all but bounded in, his smile slightly larger than usual. Elizabeth looked to Jane and noted a subtle blush rising in her cheeks. "Oh how I miss talking to Jane!"

After a few minutes of awkward conversation, Mrs. Bennet finally announced, "I feel a terrible headache coming on but I don't want to cut your visiting short! How about you young folk go for a lovely walk while I rest here? It is rather lovely today." Everyone jumped at the opportunity and before long the group had splintered predictably: Jane and Bingley, Darcy and Elizabeth, Kitty and Lydia, leaving Mr. Collins little choice but to accompany Mary.

Darcy and Elizabeth, being superior outdoorsmen soon out-stripped the others and Elizabeth led them on a path toward a lovely little copse where they could ensure privacy. Elizabeth was not even sure Jane was aware of its existence. Each was excited to fill in the other with the goings on they had missed in their respective homes. Once alone, they let down their guard and began their conversation in earnest.

"Good morning, Miss Elizabeth. How are you faring at Netherfield?"

"Well, and you Sir? How are you faring at Longbourn among so many women? How are my sisters?"

"They are well. Miss Bennet really is very nice. I don't think I have heard an unkind word from her yet - even about Miss Bingley." They both laughed. "Oh, but I wanted to talk to you about Miss Mary."

Suddenly worried, "Is she alright? She looked well enough."

"Yes, she is fine. I did not mean to worry you. It's just that your sisters and I have a plan."

Now thoroughly confused, "A plan? For Mary? To do what?"

Darcy found that despite being a little nervous he really was excited to tell her all about it, "Well, I have been watching Miss Mary around Mr. Collins." Elizabeth cringed. "Wait, hear me out. She really seems to like Mr. Collins and they are very similar in temperament and philosophies. Miss Bennet and I were discussing this, after a particularly vexing encounter between the aforementioned gentleman and myself. We realized that the solution to your problem lies with Miss Mary. She likes him; you do not. We just need to get Mr. Collins to see Miss Mary's beauty… inside and out. So, we have decided to make her over. Everyone, except your father (and of course Mary) thinks it is a marvelous idea and that is just because he is - as yet - unaware."

He seemed so proud of his scheme, and she had to admit it was rather sweet of him to take this upon himself. "How do you plan to get Mary to agree to all this? Also, if you don't mind me asking, what experience do you have dressing young women?" She smiled so he would know she was teasing.

His answer surprised her, "I often go shopping with Georgie. There are many times she is unsure of her choices in fabric or cut. I am no Beau Brummell but I am more comfortable at the modiste than your average gentleman."

"I must say I am relieved to hear that you are not another Mr. Brummell as I am quite sure I would not be able to live up to the expectations. However, with Davies' help, I think I am making a credible Mr. Darcy with your perfectly tailored clothes and charmingly disheveled hair."

Darcy couldn't help but take Elizabeth's unintended compliment to heart. It gave him hope to know she thought well of his appearance because he knew enough of her character to know if she didn't like him at all, even his appearance would be tainted by her negative opinion of his character.

"You do me more credit than I deserve, Miss Elizabeth. On the other hand, I have gained quite an education on what goes into making young ladies 'presentable.'" Rubbing his sides he smiled, continuing, "I must say my first days in a corset have made me want to do away with such a ridiculous convention! My, what you ladies suffer."

At this Elizabeth laughed aloud and held her own sides. "I can well imagine! I hate them myself. I am not sure I can resign myself to returning to the custom in the future."

It was amazing to him that they were speaking of such things but their unique situation made unique conversations inevitable For this, he was grateful.

"So, what will be your first course of action with regard to Mary?"

"Well, your mother has agreed to allow for some moderate purchases to be made updating Mary's wardrobe… if it will help secure Mr. Collins." Here he rolled his eyes dramatically but the accompanying smile assured Elizabeth that he held no truly negative feelings on the matter. "We planned a trip into Meryton to visit the modiste. Once your mother took ahold of the idea, she was quite firm that we all needed some updates to our wardrobes, especially undergarments.- that way Mr. Collins will not try to join us."

"But Sir, will you not have to actually buy undergarments… for me?"

Elizabeth looked exceedingly shy and embarrassed (a look which Darcy was sure he rarely - if ever - actually wore himself). As it dawned on him that she was correct, he sputtered, "I am sure I could just buy a night shift or something not so very… intimate."

They walked in awkward silence for a few minutes. Finally, Elizabeth - knowing she had to be the one to say something - stopped and turned to Mr. Darcy. "Sir, I am sure after the last week, we have each seen more of the other's person than either of us thought we would, even being discreet and respectful. I give you leave to buy whatever is least awkward in the moment so as not to arouse suspicion with Mama. I just ask that, as I know you are a man of honor, you continue to maintain my dignity as I will yours."

Darcy cleared his throat, unsure what he should say. He attempted to tease a smile out of her at his own expense. "So, you have seen more of me that you thought you would?"

However, it came out more intense than he meant it to. When she immediately flushed bright red, he had an idea just how much more she had seen. He stepped toward her, thinking how dearly he wished he was in his own body so he could lean down and kiss her soft, sweet lips. "I am sorry if the experience has been disagreeable, Miss Elizabeth." He said this with such a cheeky tone that she could not help think he was *flirting* with her!

"Disagreeable?" Her head buzzing from his close proximity, she could barely process his question. "Oh, no. I mean, you uh..." *Stupid, I sound like a blithering idiot. He knows I am flustered.* "Oh bother! Of course, you must know that any lady who is not blind would not think it 'disagreeable'. I will not pretend otherwise." Exasperated and still a little embarrassed but determined not to be missish, Elizabeth threw her hands in the air and looked Darcy in the eye.

To make peace Darcy offered, with no small embarrassment of his own, "I did not need to *be you* to be aware of your person. For every time I am near you I am drawn like a moth to a flame. To be honest, I have long found you to be distracting."

Elizabeth's breath caught at the boldness of his statement. What could he mean by being so bold? To deflect the building tension, she attempted a jest, "I thought I was 'not handsome enough to tempt you?" Though she smiled, he could see it did not reach her eyes, he knew his words had hurt her, and the mood changed.

He took her hand, "Miss Elizabeth, please know that I was in a foul humor that night because I had just left Georgie and I was loathe to be in society. It does not excuse my words but you must believe I never even looked at you when Charles suggested I dance with you or I would have seen how beautiful you truly are. Please, forgive me my foolish words."

Drawing her hand away but more from embarrassment than anger, she ran a hand through his thick hair. "Mr. Darcy, I accept your apology. For I am quite certain I owe you one of my own. I am afraid I allowed your words to color my opinion of you and I was rather vocal in my dislike. Please, forgive me as well. Then we may start anew and think only of the past as its remembrance gives us pleasure." She gave him her most sincere smile, trying to restore the easy mood they enjoyed earlier, before all the tension had set in.

Seeing this, he bowed deeply, "You are too kind, Madame." And a smile graced his features once again.

"Oh dear, you must not bow like that! You should curtsy as you are a young lady, are you not?" Relieved, Elizabeth teased, "Let me see you try. I would hate to think you may be disgracing me all over town with a flawed curtsy."

****

All too soon they knew they must head back or risk an interrogation from the others. Upon entering the garden, they spied Jane and Bingley walking together hand in hand down the lane behind them. Nudging Elizabeth gently, Darcy said, "I don't think we have to worry. The lovebirds are just returning and from the looks of it they have news."

Of course, it was soon announced to the family that Mr. Bingley and Jane had entered into a courtship. Cheers sounded from all present and Mrs. Bennet was heard to say several times and to several people, "I knew my Jane could not be so beautiful for nothing!"

Jane approached her sister. Darcy, somewhat awkwardly, hugged her and offered sincere congratulations. Elizabeth wanted to be the one to hug Jane but knew that even sweet Jane would think it odd for Mr. Darcy to do so and instead settled for bowing over her hand saying, "Miss Bennet, you both have my best wishes." Then she backed away to let others have their chance to wish them joy. Darcy saw the brief flash of sadness but could do nothing to help. Perhaps not everything about this switch was happy, for he knew Elizabeth would keenly miss the last days with her sister before she wed if he couldn't figure out how to switch them back soon.

Chapter 15: Elizabeth

The carriage ride back to Netherfield that evening - for of course they had been invited to stay for dinner - was filled with Bingley's effusive praise for Jane, his angel, his love, his future wife. Elizabeth was more than pleased to listen to how much he loved Jane and how he couldn't wait for her to be Mistress of Netherfield - if they stayed there, and how he hoped they would have a whole passel of children, "The more the merrier, I say!"

His casual "if we stay here" gave Elizabeth pause. "You have not decided whether to stay? Don't you think you ought to discuss that with Miss Bennet? She may have strong feelings, one way or the other." She smiled, attempting to keep her tone light, "One can be too near family, I suppose."

"Of course, I plan to discuss it with Jane but you know I had originally thought to rent Netherfield with an eye to buying an estate up North in the future. Now I am not sure what we will do, though I must say I still prefer the North overall."

"You certainly are a fortunate man, Charles. Anyone with eyes can see how in love the two of you are."

"And what of you Darcy? I saw you and Elizabeth walking today. You two seem to be getting quite close. Am I to offer you congratulations soon?"

"What? No, I am sure Miss Elizabeth doesn't think of me as a potential suitor!" She was flustered that he had seen them talking. Apparently Mr. Bingley was more observant than he let on. She would have to be more careful in the future. For though she trusted his good nature, she could not risk him finding out their secret.

Bingley noted that, according to what Darcy just said, it was *Elizabeth* who did not see the potential match but he chose not to remark on it. "Darcy, do you think it would be untoward to give Jane poems that I have written, now that we are courting? It's not really like sending a letter, is it?" Bingley looked so hopeful that Elizabeth could only chuckle.

"I think she would like that very much. As long as you stick to poems - until you are engaged - you should be within the bounds of propriety." Elizabeth felt the hypocrisy of this since she and Darcy had exchanged letters and they were not courting, but there was little else to be done under the circumstances - and their letters had not been of a romantic nature.

"Do you think she will agree to be my wife? How long must we court before I may ask her?"

"Miss Bennet appears to be a very kind and sincere young lady. If she has accepted your courtship, I have no doubt she will agree to marry you. However, I think her father may not be very happy if your courtship is not at least a month in duration."

Elizabeth waited a moment, then continued, "Charles, I'm afraid I must ask you for a favor."

"You could not have picked a better time! I think I'd be willing to do almost anything at the moment, my spirits are so high!"

"I need you to speak to Caroline for me. You and I both know that I hold no affection for her beyond that afforded to her as your sister. However, her attentions toward myself are becoming impossible to ignore. I am afraid that assumptions may be made that will be damaging to both our reputations. Could you not try to find her a suitable husband? I am sure you will not want her living with you when you are married and she will soon not want to live with Louisa."

"Not want to live with Louisa? What makes you say that?"

"Er, well. I overheard Louisa telling Caroline that she and Mr. Hurst are expecting. I am sorry you found out from me. I am sure she will tell you any day now."

"Expecting? Darcy, that is fabulous! You have given me one more reason to celebrate tonight!" But seeing the panicked look on Darcy's face he stopped. "Don't worry, I will pretend I do not know! She will never know you were eavesdropping," he teased.

"I was *not* eavesdropping! They came into the library where I was reading and they didn't see me. The conversation was clearly very personal and I could not reveal myself without embarrassing them."

"I jest! It hardly matters to me. I am to be an uncle! But, to your earlier question… I have also noticed that of late, Caroline's 'attentions' to you have become more marked. I will speak with her, encourage her to look elsewhere. I have had a few gentlemen express interest in her but I am not even sure she will look at them until you are off the market!" Rounding back to his earlier question, "Any plans in that area, old friend?"

"I… I can't say." Trying to think of any other subject to divert attention from herself, she sputtered, "For now, I would be content to not be pursued." The carriage rolled to a stop. "Congratulations, Charles. I am very happy for you, but I think I will go to bed and allow you the joy of telling your sisters the good news… alone."

Bingley rolled his eyes good naturedly, "Coward." Then called up the steps after Darcy, "Early ride tomorrow? Then maybe a visit to Longbourn?"

Smiling to herself, "Of course, Charles. Goodnight!"

A few minutes later from the safety of Darcy's room, Elizabeth heard what she could only assume was Caroline's reaction to the news. There was a crash of a glass on the floor followed by an argument. Elizabeth could not hear what was said with one major exception. As Bingley left the drawing room, he turned and shouted, "Caroline, I will not hear another word against Miss Bennet or her family or you will be sent to live with Aunt Matilda in Scotland!" Then she heard another door slam and all was quiet.

*****

Elizabeth slept soundly most nights but tonight she could not seem to fall asleep. It was clearly very late. The house was dark and quiet. Wanting a book but knowing she could not risk running into Caroline alone, she decided to have a look around Darcy's room. Though it had been over a week, she had resisted the urge to explore very much because she didn't want to 'snoop'. However, now she had little choice if she hoped to find something to help her rest.

Once out of bed, Elizabeth realized it was actually quite cold in the room. The fire was only a little low but it shouldn't be so breezy. Upon closer inspection, she found the door to the balcony was cracked open slightly. How had that occurred? She quickly took a cursory look around to make sure she was alone (as far as she knew the others were downstairs). Once satisfied that she was alone, she shut and locked the door, then checked all the windows as well. Putting on Darcy's robe to fight off the chill, she resumed her exploration. Without thought, she curled the robe around her and inhaled the masculine scent, *his* scent. Catching herself, she felt a little embarrassed but reasoned that she just liked the smell of sandalwood. It *couldn't* be because it smelled like Mr. Darcy. Could it?

As she searched the shelves for something to read, nothing caught her attention until… she saw the thick, leather bound journal sitting on the shelf near the desk. It may not be his. It could be anyone's; maybe it belonged to an ancient lord who lived at Netherfield once upon a time. She picked it up and opened it. On the first page written in a beautiful, feminine hand it read:

My beloved son,

"Let love and faithfulness never leave you;
bind them around your neck,
write them on the tablet of your heart.
Then you will win favor and a good name
in the sight of God and man."
Proverbs 3:3-4
With all my love,
Mother

Torn between curiosity and not wanting to invade his privacy (for in her heart she knew to whom it must belong), she almost put it back three times. However, she finally managed to convince herself - with the help of the brandy she had enjoyed earlier - that, *if* it was his, it might contain some very useful information. If she was supposed to act as Mr. Darcy would act, it would certainly be helpful to know how he thought. Her conscience ate at her a bit. "It will serve me right if I learn something awful." Ignoring the still, small voice in the back of her mind, she settled back into the bed to read.

The first entries were sparse and rather short; they mostly told tales of the adventures of young boys in Derbyshire. But flipping through the pages she arrived at some longer entries. As she read, her heart ached.

These were the words of a young man in despair as he watched his mother succumb to illness. He poured his heart out on paper and Elizabeth could not stop herself from reading as he described his father's rapid descent into a deep depression. While Mr. Darcy, the elder, did not die for many years, it was clear that the son felt very much alone but for Georgiana. She became the joy of young Darcy's life and he clearly worked hard to take care of her.

By the time she read of his father's death, Elizabeth was in tears. No wonder Mr. Darcy was so serious; so much had depended on him for so long. "Stupid, insolent girl. How you have misjudged him," she chided herself. She soon came across his most recent entries and stopped, afraid of what she might read.

She set the journal aside. 'It is one thing to read of the past. But it would be even more wrong to read of current events and people.' She tried to convince herself that she was not afraid to read his words about her, but she knew better. That was the crux of the issue. They had both changed due to their 'situation'. She would not want him knowing her former thoughts about him and so, she would not read his thoughts about her.

With her resolve firm, she laid back and fell asleep. Her dreams were filled with the stories she had read, happy and sad. But this time, she was present in them, as herself, and there to comfort him. Suddenly the dreams changed. They were no longer of the past, they were of the future. She saw herself large with child, walking through a meadow hand in hand with *her* Mr. Darcy. He stopped and pulled her to him but as he bent his head to kiss her, everything changed again. Suddenly, it was not Mr. Darcy but Mr. Wickham that was holding her and kissing her! She clawed and pushed but she could not move him. She tried to scream but no sound came.

Looking around, frantically searching for help, she saw Miss Bingley. She reached out to her, imploring her. But Caroline just laughed. When she thought it could not be worse, Mr. Darcy took Caroline's hand and they walked away, talking and laughing as lovers do. It was then that Elizabeth noticed Caroline was large with child, while she no longer was.

Elizabeth sat bolt upright in bed. It took a moment to find her equilibrium but once she did she drew in a deep sigh of relief. "What could it mean?" Wickham had not been seen around town much since his character had become known to Mr. Bennet. In fact, he had not been welcomed anywhere in society due to Mr. Bennet's words - combined with increasing debt among local merchants. "Why should he figure in my dream?"

Elizabeth knew why Caroline had been there. But the most disturbing idea was that Caroline had somehow won Mr. Darcy over and stolen the life Elizabeth was meant to have. Wait, was that the life Elizabeth was meant to have? She could not deny how right it had felt walking with him, being in his arms, even carrying his child. She could no longer pretend, "I am in love with Mr. Darcy."

But knowing you are in love and knowing what to do about it are two very different animals. This time when Elizabeth went back to sleep, she did not dream. But she did not rest easy either.

Chapter 16: Darcy

The shopping trip had been postponed the previous day to celebrate the happy news of Jane and Bingley's courtship. However today, nothing would deter them - especially since in Mrs. Bennet's mind - she had a wedding to plan for. "It's never too early to start ordering items for your trousseau, Jane dear. Oh, I knew you could not be so beautiful for nothing!"

As the ladies walked to Meryton, the gentlemen would be fishing so there was no hurry to be back for anything until the afternoon. The ladies discussed what would need to be purchased. Occasionally Lydia had to be subtly reminded who they had devised this plan to benefit because she would become engrossed in what ribbons she *needed* for herself. While Mary, for whom the trip had been secretly planned, seemed resigned to the idea that if they must all have some new things, she would make sure to pick out the most practical items she could. The others were focused on the plan but feigned interest in their upcoming purchases. Well, all except Darcy. Try as he might he couldn't help but think that he may in fact have to purchase intimate garments for Elizabeth. Today would be torture and he would try not to enjoy every minute of it.

They arrived at the modiste at the appointed hour and began to discuss the necessary purchases. The younger girls would be getting a few basics, a new chemisette or pair of stockings. Jane, Elizabeth, of course Mary would need all new under clothes and each would get one new dress as it had been far too long and none of theirs fit the latest fashions. Mrs. Bennet exclaimed, "How am I to find them suitable husbands if they do not look their best!"

So it was that what was meant to be a simple outing for Mary, turned into a full blown shopping extravaganza. Each young lady was taken through a slew of fashion plates and fabrics and allowed to pick their favorite (moderately priced) pattern. Darcy thought to himself that once they were married, Elizabeth would have her choice of fashions - no matter the cost. It never occurred to him that he was getting rather far ahead of himself.

Once the patterns were picked out, each lady was ushered into a dressing area to be fitted. Darcy stood there, unmoving. When Mrs. Bennet saw him just standing there she said, "Come on young lady, we don't have all day." Then she started helping Elizabeth disrobe. Moments later Darcy stood there, in her undergarments and stockings looking in the mirror of the curtained off little room waiting for his turn to be fitted.

Yes, this day will be bittersweet torture. Just then, Mrs. Bennet returned - he had not even noticed she'd left - with a new pair of stockings, corset, and shift. "Here, put these on so they can measure you when they are done with Jane." Then just as quickly, she left again to take similar items to Mary. There was nothing else but to do as she said. So one by one he removed the old, cotton stockings he had carefully put on only this morning.

He picked up the new stockings. These too were simple cotton and Darcy longed for the day when he could give Elizabeth the best. He took a stocking in his hand and slowly slid it up her leg and onto her thigh, fastening the garters in place; then the other. Looking in the mirror he imagined Elizabeth dressing in *their* room at Pemberley.

Next, he removed her the corset and shift to replace them with the new ones. Before he did however, he stopped arrested by the sight of her, naked except for the aforementioned stockings. It took his breath away. She was so beautiful and alluring. Just as he reverently reached up to touch her skin, he heard Mrs. Bennet rustling toward the room. He quickly put on the rest of the undergarments left by Mrs. Bennet and turned toward the door.

Noting the flush of Lizzy's skin and the almost confused look in her eyes, Mrs. Bennet became concerned. "Are you quite alright child? You look unwell."

"No Mama, I … I think I just need some air. Perhaps once I have been fitted, I can step outside whilst you and Jane attend to Mary?"

Almost absentmindedly, Mrs. Bennet, who had already begun draping fabrics across Elizabeth, said, "I'm sure that will be fine." Then she grumbled, "You are just here to further the plan, anyway. You should be grateful to Jane for convincing me of this little scheme. I know it was probably all your idea, young lady. Let us hope it works."

'Yes, let us hope indeed,' he thought to himself.

******

Darcy stepped out of the shop almost an hour later, promising he would just run across the way to the general store and return shortly. Walking alone and deep in thought, Darcy was quite surprised to be joined by George Wickham.

"Good afternoon, Miss Elizabeth. You are looking well."

Darcy did not acknowledge Wickham hoping he would go away. However, to his surprise, Wickham kept a jovial countenance but very quietly sneered, "Do you not know that your father's lies have made me a pariah? I had thought we were becoming quite good friends." His tone insinuated much more than friendship. Moving so that he blocked her path without appearing overtly threatening to others, he added, "Is this is how you treat your friends, Miss Elizabeth? By spreading rumors? Perhaps I need to teach you some manners. I think I would quite like that!"

Darcy looked around, noting that no one was in earshot but that all it would take was a loud shriek to bring them running. He turned to Wickham and pointed Elizabeth's dainty finger into his chest. "I think you have mistaken me for someone else Lt. Wickham. You seem to think I am fooled by your false charm. You may have the appearance of a gentleman but you are nothing more than a degenerate gambler and a rake! If you are foolish enough to approach me or my sisters again, I will happily make you like one of our steers at Longbourn. I am not a shrinking violet, Lt. Wickham. Now I suggest you move."

Wickham was so stunned, he did as he was commanded. Without another word, Darcy lifted his chin and walked with purpose toward his destination. 'How dare that bounder approach, much less threaten, her! This will not be borne. I have dealt with his malicious behavior long enough.' How he would do it, he was not sure but he would be rid of Wickham for good this time. 'I cannot allow him to hurt anyone else.'

*****

Returning to the modiste less than 20 minutes later, Darcy felt sufficiently composed. He found Jane and Kitty looking at some reticule patterns and enquired as to the success with Mary. "Has she found anything she likes? I truly hope she is enjoying herself."

"Actually," Jane replied looking around to make sure she was not overheard, "Mama has been fawning over poor Mary and I think she is unsure how to handle it. Now that Mama sees her as the next Mistress of Longbourn, she seems to have developed a fondness for her."

"I must say, the last pattern she tried only needed a very little tailoring to be quite fetching. I think if she will let us sweep her hair away from her face and put maybe a touch of rouge she will really be quite pretty." Kitty spoke rather animatedly, using hand gestures to illustrate the cut of the dress and how she'd like to fashion Mary's hair.

Kitty's excitement caught Lydia's eye from across the room and she decided to join in the conversation. "She will never be beautiful as my Jane (imitating Mrs. Bennet with surprising accuracy) but she looks a sight better than before!"

"Lydia, that is uncharitable of you! Everyone has their own beauty. You would do well to focus less on outer appearances. Mary's already developed her inner beauty, now we are just helping her match it on the outside," Jane admonished.

The three ladies spent another 30 minutes talking and accessorizing their new outfits. It would be at least a week before the dresses would be done. However, they would begin re-trimming their bonnets as soon as they got home. Suddenly Darcy realized that he was utterly incapable of trimming a bonnet. Perhaps he could sneak some of the needed materials out with him on his walks and then Elizabeth could teach him some basics when they met. Ha! If Georgie could see him now!

Chapter 17

Elizabeth

Elizabeth woke with the sun despite a considerable lack of sleep. She had planned to meet Darcy early for another tete-a-tete but she knew that he and her sisters would be shopping today. So instead, Elizabeth decided to go for a ride because that is what Darcy would likely have done. If she got nervous riding, she could always just walk beside Hector or let him graze while she read.

On her way to the stable she noticed some of the maids scurrying about taking hot bricks, extra blankets, as well as a carafe of hot tea to Miss Bingley's room. Elizabeth was not particularly concerned but nevertheless thought it best ask after her health, just in case. *Keep your friends close…* she thought to herself.

She was hurriedly informed that Caroline had somehow managed to lock herself out on her balcony last night - very late - and had not been discovered for almost an hour when her maid came to stoke the fire in her room. They "would not be surprised if she caught her death out there." What no one could figure out was why Caroline had been out so late and how she managed to get locked out.

Elizabeth was horrified to realize that Caroline must have known that Darcy's balcony was unlocked. But how would she have gotten to from hers to his? There was no easy way to climb in. No, she must have been planning to sneak into Darcy's room before he went up to bed but then Elizabeth had gone to bed early and ruined that option. Had Caroline been outside looking for another way in? How would she have known his door had been left unlocked? She must have help from someone who has access to both rooms. But who?

Remembering the other events of last night, Elizabeth felt a little ashamed of herself for having read Darcy's journal. She had let the few drinks she had had after dinner affect her. But she also could not deny that a part of her was glad she had read it. For now she understood Mr. Darcy on a deeper level. She just hoped he wouldn't be too angry with her. She would have to tell him. She just didn't know how. Now that she understood her own feelings, every interaction with Mr. Darcy meant more.

Arriving at the stable, she exchanged pleasantries with Henry as he readied Hector. "Good morning, Henry. How are the horses treating you?"

"Oh fine, Sir! No place I'd rather be than out here with these four-legged beasts. Me sister, she's a maid up at the house and she thinks herself so high and mighty because she thinks she's going to work her way up to ladies' maid someday. But not me, I already have the best job. I'm out of doors, exercising these brutes…."

Elizabeth lost track of Henry's ramblings. She hadn't realized his sister, Jeana, worked at Netherfield. Perhaps she would be of some help? But how to approach her? It would have been awkward to have done so as herself, much more so as Mr. Darcy. What would a gentlemen like him need to speak with a maid for? She'd have to keep an eye out for opportunities to do so without making anyone suspicious.

As she rode away toward the open fields on the far side of the estate, Elizabeth thought she saw a man sneaking away from the kitchen entrance. It was still quite early for deliveries to be made but perhaps it was one of the gardeners running late and hoping to avoid detection. Or it could be a lover of one of the servants. Either way, perhaps she ought to say something to Mr. Bingley. Oh how she wished she could just go home!

****

Elizabeth spent the morning riding, slowly, across the countryside, deep in thought. So much had changed in her world in the short time since the Netherfield Ball. She now knew - beyond a shadow of a doubt - that she had misjudged both Mr. Darcy and Lt. Wickham. The men had more than reversed roles in her mind. For even at the height of her disdain for Mr. Darcy - when she thought he had mistreated Lt. Wickham, she never once considered him to be so wholly corrupt as she now knew Lt. Wickham to be. "How could I have ever considered having feelings for Wickham?"

The problem she now faced was, even if she told Mr. Darcy of her feelings (ridiculous), there was no guarantee he would feel the same way. He had certainly been flirting with her yesterday but perhaps it was just the odd situation they were in that was causing him to pay her these attentions. Despite his protests to the contrary, she was quite certain he had not always held her in the esteem he seemed to now. He may think her pretty but that did not mean he thought she was a suitable choice to make his wife.

After some time, she turned Hector back toward Netherfield. She still found that the clean, crisp air of the country helped clear her mind better than anything else and she would need to be at her best for today's excursion. Darcy, Bingley, and Hurst were going to go fishing with her father at her favorite lake on Longbourn.

Her father knew her better than anyone in the world, save Jane, and she was not sure she would be able to fool him for an extended period of time. Fortunately, the idea of Mr. Darcy in fact, not being Mr. Darcy would probably never cross his mind. He might, however, begin to think something was amiss and she didn't want to do anything to harm Jane and Bingley's chance at happiness - or further cause her father to dislike Mr. Darcy.

She knew she'd done some damage to Mr. Darcy's reputation with her father after the assembly. Now she hoped that she could make him see that she'd been mistaken and that Mr. Darcy was, in fact, an honorable man. Today, her mission would be to do just that.

****

Upon her return, Elizabeth found that Mr. Bingley and Mr. Hurst were almost ready to depart for their fishing expedition. "Sorry gentlemen, I must have lost track of the time. I will be down shortly." Then she took the stairs two at a time (a simple act of freedom that her mother did not allow because it was not 'lady-like').

The gentlemen had planned to meet at the lake. Mr. Bennet and Mr. Collins were already there when the Netherfield party arrived but Mr. Bennet quickly waved away all attempts at apologies for being late. "I like getting the lay of the land before I start, so I arrived early."

Throughout the morning and early afternoon, the gentlemen vacillated between silent contemplation and easy small talk. The beauty of fishing is that one only has to talk when and if they desire to and, often, silence is preferred. Mr. Bennet had directed for luncheon to be served outside and so when the servants arrived with baskets of cucumber sandwiches, biscuits, tarts, sweet meats and carafes of hot, lemon tea the men eagerly gathered around the picnic blankets.

Elizabeth, wanting to maintain a friendly banter, asked after everyone's success? "Mr. Bennet? Are the fish biting for you, Sir? I thought I spied you stripping the line for a rather large trout earlier?"

A gentle smile graced Mr. Bennet's face. "Ah, yes! I have a caught a couple good sized fish but the catch of the day for me will likely be the last one I managed to reel in. He was easily 18 inches!"

Mr. Collins spoke up, extolling the virtues of fishing even though he had not managed to catch a single fish. "Perhaps there is a problem with my equipment."

Elizabeth had to look away and stifle a laugh, for there was indeed much wrong with Mr. Collins' equipment. So much so that she doubted he had ever been fishing before.

Attempting to redirect the conversation, Bingley interjected, "Wow, that's a marvelous catch! And I thought I had caught the trophy of the day at a mere 15 inches! How did you lot manage?" Bingley asked looking from Mr. Darcy to Mr. Hurst.

Hurst joked that while he had caught a handful, they were all fairly small but would taste just fine sautéed with a little lemon and butter!"

"And you, Mr. Darcy? How have you fared today?" Mr. Bennet asked. Elizabeth noticed that Mr. Bennet had watched her carefully most of the morning and figured he must be trying to better understand Mr. Darcy. She hoped he was coming to a positive conclusion.

"Well, Sir. I had a little trouble early on. I am sure you could not have failed to see me get my line snagged a couple times." They all chuckled for they *had* seen Darcy lose more than one hook. But if he was willing to acknowledge it with good humor, they felt safe to laugh. "However, I did manage to land a couple keepers."

After tea, they fished for another hour or so before deciding to head back to Longbourn. The ladies should be back soon and Mr. Bennet decided to invite the party to stay for dinner. "I hear there may be fresh fish on the menu," he said with a wink.

Mr. Hurst thanked Mr. Bennet for the wonderful fishing but had to beg forgiveness for not being able to join the party for a meal. He then announced that, "Mrs. Hurst and I are expecting and she has not been feeling well on account of the babe. I'd like to go check in on her. Especially since Caroline is under the weather, I don't want her to eat alone."

This of course met with some gentle teasing but, in truth, they all would have made the same decision if in his place - and said so. Then they all gave their congratulations and bid him good day. Elizabeth was again moved to hear the men express such a sweet sentiments.

By the time the fishing party made it back to the house, the ladies had indeed returned. As the men entered the parlor, the ladies were clearly in raptures over their purchases. Mary had even let Kitty do her hair and Elizabeth thought she looked quite pretty. She noticed that as soon as Mr. Collins walked in the room, Mary blushed a little but made eye contact with him nonetheless and he walked over and greeted her. While there was no obvious flirting, it was encouraging to see the interaction between the two and the fact that he had barely given Elizabeth a glance.

Jane and Bingley had immediately moved to a corner of the room to talk quietly, Kitty and Lydia were still gushing over ribbons, so that made it very easy for Elizabeth to join Darcy who, she noticed, had conveniently sat in the window seat again - far enough to be out of earshot of others without appearing to desire privacy.

Elizabeth laughed quietly when she saw what Darcy had been working on. His (or rather her) fingers were bloodied a little from needles and her bonnet was in tatters. "Fortunately that was already my least favorite bonnet." She said with a smile.

Darcy grinned in return, relieved. "Oh please, take pity on me and lend me your expert opinion. Where am I going wrong?"

"Oh, where to begin?" Taking the bonnet in hand, she examined his attempts. "Well first of all, you're using the wrong thread. You need a heavier thread so that it will hold up in the wind."

"Do you think... would it be too much to ask to meet me tomorrow in the copse so we can work on it?" He asked, his tone full of hope.

"I think it may be the only way to save the bonnet!" She smiled and they both laughed quietly, hoping not to attract attention. But it was too late for Mr. Bennet had been quietly observing them both since the dinner at Lucas Lodge. He had to admit, he liked Darcy well enough and it was clear Elizabeth had changed her opinion of him. But was this the man who would claim the heart of his favorite child? If so, he had to be sure of his character.

Chapter 18: Darcy

Darcy awoke feeling awful. He felt lethargic and irritable. As he gathered his things to meet Elizabeth, he could think of no reason why he should be under the weather. He was just about to head down stairs when he felt it, he felt… wet? 'Oh for the love of all that is good and holy, please don't let this be what I think it is.'

He walked over to his dressing table, picked up the hand towel and - with no small amount of dread and embarrassment - wiped… down there. Inspecting towel, his fears were confirmed. But Elizabeth had said it would be weeks before her menses returned. Now he was sure this whole situation was a cosmic joke. He had somehow offended the gods and was now paying the price.

After doing his best to clean up quickly, he began to look around for Elizabeth's feminine cloths. At least, he hoped she'd have some readily available for those were the only thing he was familiar with (because that is what Mrs. Reynolds had given Georgie to use a few years ago). "Ah ha! Found them!"

Taking a napkin in his hand he turned it over. 'Why is there a string attached?' Then he saw the belt-like contraption sitting next to the cloths. It appeared to hold the cloth in place when one attached it to the belt with the strings. That had to be it.

After a few minutes of arranging and rearranging, Darcy was sure it was still not right. But as everyone else was still asleep, it would have to do until he could locate the book Elizabeth had spoken of. Grabbing an extra cloth, or two (how many of these are needed?), he put them in his reticule and he went downstairs. On his way out, he stopped by the kitchen and grabbed a biscuit and an apple, then added another biscuit.

Walking toward the copse, Darcy couldn't help but be a little sad. He had originally planned to tell Elizabeth of his feelings. But now, it just didn't *feel* right. He felt foolish. It was not like anything had changed. He still loved her beyond what he thought possible and he hoped that she felt - if not the love - growing affection for him. The other day they had been so close. His stomach fluttered just remembering it.

But today, he felt like he would just bungle it if he tried to tell her how he felt. Not to mention, he felt utterly unattractive. Which he knew to be ridiculous because, objectively, Elizabeth was as beautiful as ever. 'Is this how women feel *every* month?' He hadn't had any of the intense physical pain he had often heard of and he prayed to God for mercy. Was this meant to make him a better brother, husband, father; develop empathy? While he could not imagine a more effective method, he could certainly think of less dramatic ones.

Rounding the last bend in the path, he saw her. She looked deep in thought, pacing back and forth. Hector heard him before she did and bristled, alerting Elizabeth to his presence. When their eyes met, she smiled.

"Good morning, Sir. Did you bring the bonnet? I have some ideas that I believe may salvage it."

He smiled and returned her greeting, "Ah yes. I did." Still smiling he handed her the bonnet then he set down the small bag of ribbons and sewing tools on the picnic blanket she had already spread. There was an awkward silence as they both sat. Darcy got out the food he had brought so Elizabeth did the same.

After another minute, she asked, "Mr. Darcy, is everything alright? You seem… distracted."

Grimacing he said nothing for a moment. Then he decided there was no reason to hide his situation from her. A little embarrassed, he said, "Well, actually Miss Elizabeth, it seems I will be the first man in history to have the *FULL* female experience."

She looked at him for a minute before it dawned on her what he meant. Then, despite considerable effort, uncontrollable laughter burst forth. Still laughing, "I'm sorry. I don't mean to laugh, it's just that… women have always wished that just once a man would have to suffer through what we do! It seems, our wishes have come true."

Darcy sat there, chagrined but not upset. "Lucky me."

"Oh you poor dear! Did you find the supplies you need? "

He patted the reticule beside him. "May I ask what I can expect? It is clear that I will be irritable and feel a general malaise."

"Well, in addition to that you will likely begin cramping soon. It should be intermittent and last a couple days. I am among the fortunate ones for I have never experienced severe nausea and my cramps have always been relatively mild. Poor Jane is debilitated for almost a full week."
At this Darcy raised his hand, "I do not need to know about Jane, or any of your sisters, please." Realizing how harsh he sounded, he apologized. "Forgive me. I did not mean to be gruff. I am not myself." At this, they both smiled.

"Never has a truer statement been made, Sir. However, I think you will handle it admirably." Continuing her list of what he should expect, she added, "I have always found that walking helps. Though, it will be the last thing you will want to do. You will want to stay curled up in bed… and cry for no reason." At his horrified expression, she laughed again.

They sat together working to retrim her bonnet. Elizabeth - with great patience - taught Darcy the basics of bonnet trimming so he could do a passable job if called to do so in the future. More than once their hands touched and each felt a jolt when they did but neither commented on it.

Darcy, cursed his circumstances but was forced to admit that if *he* felt unattractive and unable to voice his feelings, it was likely

Elizabeth would not have been in a place to hear them had their situation not been reversed. He was pulled from his musings when Elizabeth gasped, "Mr. Darcy, I just remembered! Miss Bingley is ill because - and I may be jumping to conclusions - she got locked out of her room – on the balcony - whilst trying to find a way into yours."

"Oh dear God!"

"Do not worry yourself; nothing came of it. I woke up in the middle of the night due to the cold of your room, when I noticed the balcony door had been left open. I believe she had planned to sneak in at some point and lay in wait. However, I locked the door before returning to bed so she was unsuccessful. It doesn't really make sense though. I am still working it out."

"It is quite simple actually. I should have thought to warn you but I didn't think she knew. You see, I have discovered several passages in the house. None led into my room, thankfully, but I know there is one in the room next to mine. I'd be willing to wager that Miss Bingley was going to use it to sneak downstairs unseen from her room." Thinking aloud he continued, "From there, it would not be a difficult climb from that balcony to mine."

"The maid said, she had been locked out on *her* balcony."

"Perhaps they were mistaken or perhaps they are attempting to cover it up. But I am surprised she knows of the secret passages. She is not exactly the curious, exploring type. Do you think she has help?"

"I do. How else could she be assured your door would be unlocked? It must be someone very familiar with the home." Elizabeth secretly enjoyed having a mystery they had to solve together. She just wished that there wasn't so much riding on their success.

Taking her hand, Darcy looked deep into her eyes, "Please Elizabeth, our… I mean, err, *my* future happiness depends on not allowing her to trap me into marriage."

Did he just use her Christian name? He did, and Elizabeth found that she liked it. Swallowing, she realized her mouth was suddenly very dry. "I promise you, Mr. Darcy, I won't let anything happen."

Chapter 19: Darcy

The next few days went by slowly. A storm blew in from the North bringing with it the first snow of winter. Unfortunately, it was mixed with sleet resulting in a bitter cold and impassable roads. So it was that Darcy spent his days bundled in the window seat, curled up with a book, quite miserable, and fully feeling the effects of a woman's monthly flow.

Several times, Kitty or Jane had attempted to pull him into their conversations without luck. He tried his best not to be quarrelsome but when on the third day, he overheard Mr. Collins suggest to Mary that he was "pouting because she didn't get to go play outside" he almost snapped. With all the restraint he could muster, Darcy chose to ignore Mr. Collins and 'rejoice' in the fact that he and Mary seemed to be becoming quite close. It seemed their plan was having the intended effect.

Kitty entered the parlor just then, practically bouncing with excitement. "I thought we could all use a little treat after being stuck in this house for so long so I asked cook if she would help me make hot chocolate and biscuits"

"Oh how thoughtful," Jane exclaimed, genuinely excited.

Lydia squealed, "Hot chocolate? Oh Kitty, I knew I there was a reason I loved you best!" Then giggling at Mary and Mr. Collin's disapproving looks, she got up to help serve.

Even Mr. and Mrs. Bennet came in for the treat. Darcy looked around and realized it was not often that all the Bennets (and Collins) sat in one room and enjoyed each other's company.

"We should play a game! Snap Dragon! Or charades!"

Mr. Bennet spoke up, "Tsk, tsk, Lydia. We are already enjoying hot chocolate. We'll save the raisins for closer to Christmas."

Undeterred she tried again, "How about Pass the Slipper? It may be a child's game but it is fun. Or Shades!"

"Ooh Shades! I'll get the paper and lamp black!" Jane said as she actually jumped up and left the room.

"I'll get the candles," Kitty said opening the cupboard.

As they all gathered around preparing to play. Darcy looked up and saw Mr. Bennet attempting to sneak away. "Oh no you don't, Papa! I plan to sketch you first!" As Darcy took Mr. Bennet's arm and gently pulled him back into the room, the older gentleman looked chagrined but said,

"If you must, but I expect a game of chess later to make up for subjecting me to this tom foolery."

"With pleasure, Papa."

So they took turns standing and tracing each other's outlines. Some, like Lydia, took great pleasure making the outlines exaggerated and grotesque. Others like Mary - who outlined Mr. Collins - were more serious, though with not much better results. As promised, Darcy outlined Mr. Bennet and even he was pleased with how it turned out.

"Why Lizzy, I may have to frame this and place it in my study to add a sense of decorum." Though he teased, Darcy knew Mr. Bennet would likely do just that because his Lizzy had made it. For a brief moment remembering how his father had been much the same with him pained him but he quickly shook it off to enjoy the reverie.

"Lizzy, it is my turn to do you!" Jane said turning to Darcy. "Come on, now. You're the last one."

Darcy stood still as Jane, took her time. When she was sure no one was paying attention Jane whispered, "Perhaps Lizzy, one day you can give this to Mr. Darcy."

Darcy blushed and Jane immediately clarified, "Not now, goose. But if he ever declares himself to you... I know you like him, despite your protestations to the contrary. Mr. Bingley and I think it would be perfect. We could move up North, near Pemberley, and our children could play together." She waxed on for another moment as they both became lost in the picture she painted of the future. "Well, I finished. What do you think?"

"Oh Jane, its perfect." He said quite taken with her work. "It looks just like… me."

"Well of course it does! Here, now drink your chocolate before it gets cold and I will set these out to dry."

They spent the rest of the afternoon with various members of the family playing games such as Charades or Spillikins, reading, and occasionally playing on the pianoforte. All in all, it was a very pleasant afternoon and Darcy found, to his delight, that he had not once found himself wishing to escape above stairs.

That evening before bed, Darcy thought more about Jane's description of their perfect futures. It sounded so wonderful. He just hoped that Elizabeth would think so too.

****

At Netherfield, tensions had been high for the past few days as Caroline's health had not yet improved. Elizabeth noted maids going to and from her room at all hours of the day and night. Approaching Charles in his study one night after dinner - the second night in a row Caroline had not attended, Elizabeth asked, "Charles, how is Caroline's health? Has there been any improvement?"

Charles poured himself a full brandy and offered one to Elizabeth. But she declined remembering the effects from the last time. He shrugged before slumping into a chair by the fire.

"I'm scared Darcy. Her fever hasn't broken and the doctor says there is no more to be done but wait for her to fight through."

Elizabeth crossed the room and sat in the opposing chair. "Caroline is nothing if not a fighter, Charles. I've never seen determination like hers."

Charles looked up and seeing Darcy smiling gently, he chuckled. "I suppose you're right."

"I am. You'll see. She will be up and around in no time."

"I hope so. I know you two have your differences but she is still my sister. I don't know what I'd have done if she hadn't always been there to push me. She really does care, deep, deep… deep down."

Elizabeth was pretty sure that Caroline had always pushed because it benefited her to do so. But that didn't matter when it came to brotherly love. Charles' feelings were genuine and to his credit.

"Come Charles, let's go play billiards. It does no one any good to borrow trouble. Besides, it should be drying up soon and you will be able to visit your Miss Bennet."

With a knowing look, Charles smiled, "And you, *yours*. You cannot fool me Darcy. I have known you for a long time, old friend, and I have never seen you this way before. Tell me, have you an understanding with Miss Elizabeth?"

Answering honestly, "No, we do not. I have feelings but I am not sure they are returned."

At this Charles, laughed heartily. "Not returned? I say, perhaps in the beginning they were not but I have watched you two." Seeing the doubt in his friend's eyes, he continued, "I know you think I am lost in my amour, but I tell you, friend, if you cannot see what I have seen clear as day… you are blind indeed!"

They played billiards into the early hours of the morning. Before heading up to bed, Elizabeth decided to run down to the kitchen for a late night snack. Hoping not to disturb anyone, she tiptoed down the stairs and into the larder looking for a quick bite to eat.

Hearing footsteps approach and not wanting to be discovered she quickly pulled the doors to. There were two voices: one male and one female and neither were completely unfamiliar. As she listened it dawned on her who she was hearing. The male voice was undoubtedly Lt. Wickham. The female voice she was not sure of but thought it might be Jeana - the stable boy's sister. She had not spoken to Jeana in many years but she often saw her at church so she wasn't a complete stranger.

She heard giggling, "Shhh, George. You shouldn't be here."

"How can I resist such temptations, my dear? You are too much."

More giggling from her and soft moans from him. Elizabeth could only assume they were kissing. *Odious, disgusting rake! I'm going to be sick*. But what she heard a few minutes later made her blood run cold.

"So, when shall we hear of the announcement? I bet, his face was priceless when he woke up to see her next to him in bed. He always was such a prude."

"Oh, George, don't be mad. He woke up before she made it over the balcony and he locked his door without ever seeing her. And I already locked the guestroom door and rushed out so no one would find me. At first I thought maybe he had welcomed her to his bed, so I didn't want to disturb them. But when I went back to 'catch them' nearly an hour later, she was not there. I checked the guest balcony only to find her froze half to death! I snuck her back upstairs and told everyone she had gotten locked out of her room. Oh Lord, I hope she doesn't die!"

Jeana was nearly in tears but Wickham didn't seem to care. "You daft cow! How can you mess up such a fool-proof plan?" He pushed her away and paced the kitchen. "All my life, Darcy has had everything I ever wanted. I finally have a chance at revenge and you bungle it up. I should have known a half-wit maid could never pull this off. You better hope, the fancy miss keeps her mouth shut."

"George, please don't say that. I thought you loved me!" She pleaded with him, "We are going to have a baby. You said, you'd marry me and take me away from here. Make me an officer's wife."

He laughed cruelly. "Why is it you women all believe the same old lines? Of course, I'm not going to marry you. Why would I marry a *maid* with no money? I am a *gentleman* after all," he sneered. And with that he turned and walked out the way he came in. Stopping at the door, he said, "Don't worry, sweetie, I'll find another way to get my revenge. I've never been a quitter."

Jeana picked up an apple and lobbed it at his head, narrowly missing. Wickham laughed again and left, never looking back. It was another hour before Elizabeth could sneak back to Darcy's room as Jeana had slumped to the ground crying for some time. As much as she wanted to, Elizabeth knew she couldn't comfort her. Even if she had been herself, Jeana would never have wanted anyone else to know.

Chapter 20: Elizabeth

Elizabeth awoke with a start. Someone was banging loudly at her door. She looked to see Davies already moving to answer it. It was evidently quite early if Davies had not been up yet. Elizabeth stood and put on a robe, then nodded to Davies. Bingley practically burst into the room but seeing nothing amiss he stopped short, confused.

"Charles? What brings you to my room so early?"

"You were screaming. I went to check on Caroline and on my way to breakfast I heard you. Are you alright? Is something troubling you?"

"Huh? No. Well, yes, but I can work it out. I have been having terrible nightmares. I apologize for worrying you." She invited him in and they sat by the fire for a minute in silence. Seeing that Bingley looked haggard, she inquired, "Any improvement with Caroline?"

Looking up from the fire, Bingley seemed to gather his wits. "Her fever broke last night but the doctor says she has an infection in her lungs. If she can get past that, she will recover but will likely be weak for some time. Maybe even require nursing. I don't know what to do. Louisa is expecting and I hope to be newlywed soon." He paused to make sure Darcy comprehended the issue.

"And you are not sure who Caroline should stay with?"

"Yes, that's it exactly! It's not fair to Jane to have to nurse my sister but neither should Louisa have to worry over her when she will have a new baby to care for. Louisa suggested sending Caroline to Aunt Matilda's for a time but I hardly think that is fair."

Lightning struck in Elizabeth's mind and she began to formulate a plan. "I have an idea. It may seem odd but hear me out."

Elizabeth went on to explain what she had overheard while in the larder closet and her plan. At first Bingley could only focus on the idea that Caroline had tried to compromise his friend.

"You mean to tell me that she lies in bed, fighting for her life because of her greed? Does Louisa know of this?" He was stomping more than pacing and Elizabeth had never seen Bingley so angry. She doubted Darcy had either.

"It is unlikely that Caroline confided in anyone about her plans."

Bingley seemed mollified a bit by that. "So, despite how this maid would have helped trap you into marriage, you'd have me help her? Why?"

"She is young and was manipulated. Wickham can be very persuasive and I think she thought if he didn't fulfill his word, at least she would have a place in Miss Bingley's service. Either way, she is in need and I feel obligated, having not thought to warn you or your staff."

"Why did you not make your presence known? Demand he marry her?"

"I wouldn't wish him on anyone. Being forced into marriage would not have made him honorable and she (and her child) would have suffered for it."

"True. I suppose what you suggest could work. Caroline won't like it."

"So much the better. I do not wish her ill but I think it is high time she is put in her place."

"I will write to Aunt Matilda today. I think you have the right of it."

Bingley left with a plan, determined to see it through, and Elizabeth got up to dress for the day.

As Davies set about readying her clothes, Elizabeth headed for the privy. "Ugh, I will never get used to this. Men are so…

odd. I have to pee and yet I cannot because *he* is practically standing at attention. Ok, think of something unappealing." After a few minutes, the issue subsided and she was able to relieve herself.

"Men, even when there is no reason. Hmph."

******

Seeing that the weather had finally let up, Elizabeth was practically itching to get outside and she was willing to bet Darcy felt the same. He should be nearly over his... 'ailment' by now. She laughed remembering the helpless look on his face. Poor man.

After grabbing a quick bite to eat, she looked in on Bingley who was now working on some papers in his study. "I'm going for a ride." And before Bingley could protest, she added, "I'll be back in time to call on the Bennets!" With that, she headed for the stables.

"Good morning, Hector! It is a lovely day for a ride. You can hardly tell it snowed the other day!" No one else seemed to be around but Elizabeth didn't mind. She hadn't told them she'd ride out today and they were probably busy exercising the other horses after such foul weather. Hector nosed her by way of greeting and she was soon on her way.

She rode to the copse but Darcy was not there. Then she rode to Oakham Mount. As she crested the peak, she saw him, laying in the grass, hands behind his head, with his eyes closed. He looked so peaceful that she thought he must be asleep.

Elizabeth quietly dismounted Hector so as not to disturb Darcy and crept over toward him until she was kneeling next to him, when an idea struck her. "I wonder if he is as ticklish as I? I mean now that he is me, he should be… right?" Holding her hands in the air just above his armpits, she looked around once more to make sure they were not being observed. She knew this was the height of impropriety but she could not resist. When she looked back, she noticed his eyes were open and looking upon her with great amusement. Before she could react, he grabbed her, pulled her to the ground, and was up in a flash tickling *her*.

She 'fought' back trying to tickle him as they both collapsed into fits of laughter. "You thought to take advantage of an innocent, young maiden now did you, Miss Elizabeth?" Darcy could barely catch his breath as he teased her.

Elizabeth answered in shorts bursts, "Me? No Sir, I believe you made the first move!"

"Preposterous! You snuck up and if I had not heard you - you really are not as graceful when you are so large - you would have had me at your mercy!"

They sat there staring at each other's leaf covered clothes and hair. "Oh dear, what will you tell Mama when you get home?" She smiled, picking a leaf out of the curls now falling from their pins.

"Simple, I will just explain that I was not careful - as usual - and fell on a slippery patch. Apparently, you are known to be a bit clumsy. I never would have guessed, Miss Elizabeth." Chuckling, he leaned toward her, and reached to help her straighten his jacket. He was so close he could feel her breath hitch. When he looked at her, their eyes locked. He moved closer, his eyes dropping to her lips, he lifted one hand to her cheek, and then the other. This was not how he had imagined kissing Elizabeth but he didn't care anymore. He had to know if she felt the same. He looked in her eyes again as if asking for permission. Her almost imperceptible nod was enough.

It started slow but before long they each, simultaneously, rose on their knees in an effort to get closer. Elizabeth ran her hands up his neck and his hair. He reveled in the feelings that coursed through her body. He wanted to memorize them so he could use that knowledge to ensure her pleasure in the future. He felt her chest tighten and her nipples go taut. He felt her stomach quiver and her knees weaken, and everything in between ache. *Oh sweet mercy.*

For Elizabeth's part, she was so lost in the new sensations that she could hardly register the changes that occurred in his body until they touched. Then it was all she could feel. Their bodies pressed against each other; it was agonizing and blissful at the same time. All she wanted was more. More contact, more movement.

When he pulled back, she groaned in protest. He just smiled. "It is nice to *know* you are affected by me much as I am by you. But we cannot continue. Not like this. Not here. I want you Elizabeth, but I want more than just to possess your body. I want your heart as well."

She looked at him with equal parts shame and awe. Shame because he knew she had been prepared to let things go much further (Would she if she had been herself?). Awe, because he had so openly declared his feelings. She sat on her knees across from him, wanting to tell him all that was on her heart but the words would not come.

After a moment, she just blushed and said the only words that would form, "I believe I have fallen in love with you, Fitzwilliam."

The shock on his face registered and, out of embarrassment, Elizabeth stood to leave. Her mind filled with doubts. Did she misunderstand his meaning? Maybe he wanted her but not when they could be discovered at any moment. Or maybe he just wanted to know he had her affections and now he would leave. Had he been toying with her?

She had almost made it back to Hector before Darcy caught her. "Where are you going? You can't tell me you love me and then run away!"

"But you looked so… shocked, or… I don't know. I must have misunderstood. I thought you meant…" She couldn't finish.

"That I love you? I do, Elizabeth." Taking her face in his hands he turned her so she was looking in his eyes once again. "Elizabeth, I love you more than I thought it was possible to love. Hearing you say those words did shock me. I had only hoped to earn a chance at your affections. I never suspected you returned my feelings." Then he pulled her lips to his once more. But before the kiss could deepen beyond the last of his control, he pulled back.

"You should go, my love."

Chapter 21: Darcy

Darcy sat on Elizabeth's bed lost in thought. *She loves me.* He imagined their lives together. He was sure she and Georgie would love each other. But, how could they if Georgie thought he was Elizabeth? It wouldn't be right unless they came home to Pemberley as themselves. *We have to figure this out!*

A soft knock sounded at the door. "Come in?"

Mary came into Lizzy's room with a very shy, almost worried look. "Um, Lizzy. May I speak with you a moment?"

"Of course, is something the matter?"

"Well, you see… I wanted to talk to you about Wi… I mean, Mr. Collins." Darcy smiled and Mary continued. "You see, I know at one time Mr. Collins paid you special attention and that you may be expecting a continuation of his addresses. But…"

Darcy interrupted her, "But the two of you… are becoming close?"

Relieved, "Yes, and I don't want you to be upset but, you see, I believe I may love him Lizzy! I think I have almost since he came into our home."

This was the most impassioned speech Darcy - or likely anyone - had ever heard from Mary. Pleased and yet, unable to keep himself from acting as a protective older brother, he asked, "And has Mr. Collins declared himself to you?"

She blushed and nodded. "Last night after dinner. He read to me from Ecclesiastes 4:9: "Two are better than one, because they have a good return for their labor: If either of them falls down, one can help the other up. But pity anyone who falls and has no one to help them up..." Then he told me that he could think of no more fitting partner for his future life.

Darcy noted that Collins had not read one of the many verses which included the idea of love, but he supposed each loved in his own way. Who was he to judge? Leaning forward, he hugged her. "Mary, I know you don't need me to say so but I am very happy for you. Have you told Mama yet?"

"No, he is downstairs with Papa now."

Darcy was surprised at the very real emotion he experienced for Mary. "Well," he swallowed the lump in his throat, "let me be the first to wish you joy."

Wiping tears of her own, Mary simply said, "Thank you, Lizzy." Then she left Darcy alone to his thoughts once again.

****

"Jaaaaaaaaaannnnnnnne? Lizzzzzzzzzy? Girls?? Make haste, we have visitors!" Mrs. Bennet bellowed up the stairs. As expected, Elizabeth and Bingley came at the earliest acceptable hour.

"Mr. Bingley, I have heard that your sister has been unwell. Miss Bingley that is. Pray, what ails her?" Mrs. Bennet asked with more curiosity than genuine concern but fortunately Mr. Bingley was too good to notice.

"She improves slowly, Madame. There is still some concern for her lungs but the worst appears to be over. Thank you." Without realizing it, he took a hold of Jane's hand and patted it before recollecting himself. Mrs. Bennet noticed but said nothing, taking it as a promising sign for her daughter's future happiness.

Hill entered the parlor announcing the arrival of unexpected visitors. "Lady Lucas, Miss Lucas, and Mariah Lucas, Ma'am."

Bingley, Collins, and - after a momentary lapse - Elizabeth all offered their seats to the newcomers. "Thank you, gentlemen," said Lady Lucas taking Collins' offered seat near Mrs. Bennet. Charlotte sat in the empty seat next to Darcy, allowing Elizabeth to resume her seat and her part in the conversation. Jane and Bingley removed themselves to the far corner chairs allowing the three youngest girls to occupy the couch, while Mr. Collins and Mary went to the pianoforte where he turned the pages whilst she played.

"Have you heard, Mrs. Bennet? It seems that Lt. Wickham is a rake as well as a gambler. There is rumor that he has gotten several young ladies 'in the family way'. Oh mostly poor, young women who have no one to protect them. It is really quite a vulgar business!"

"Thank goodness Mr. Bennet made Wickham's character known to you or who knows what might have happened! He might have preyed on your poor Charlotte!"

"Mama!" Jane and Darcy exclaimed. "Charlotte is hardly without protection."

"And I hope I would have better judgement that to be taken in by a rake such as Lt. Wickham!" Charlotte did not appear offended but Elizabeth could not help but be embarrassed. "Anyway, it is too late for Lt. Wickham as I find myself happily engaged to Mr. Paulson, Mr. Townsend's nephew."

Several of the ladies squealed in delight and Elizabeth had to bite her tongue not to beg for more information. However, seeing her eager looks, Darcy spoke up. "How and when did you meet, Charlotte?"

"Well, you see Mr. Paulson came to Meryton from Keswick to help his uncle run the bookshop. You know Mrs. Townsend has been ill and they are moving to Bath. So, Mr. Paulson will take over. We met quite by chance. I was crossing the street when a carriage, driving much too fast, almost ran me over. I dropped all my parcels, and Mr. Paulson - who saw the whole incident - ran out from the bookshop to assist me. We started talking and …"

"And he has visited every day for the past two weeks! Well, except during that dreadful storm this last week." Lady Lucas rarely interrupted people, but since she was clearly so elated at her daughter's news, no one could fault her.

Mrs. Bennet was not as elated as Lady Lucas but offered her begrudging congratulations. She had wanted to marry her daughters off before Lady Lucas and for a while it looked like that might be the case. However close Jane was to being engaged, it was not official so Mrs. Bennet could not brag about her advantageous match just yet.

Mr. Collins looked hopefully at Mary for approval but before she could agree or disagree, he was already standing and calling everyone's attention. "Excuse me, in light of the happy news… I would like to make an announcement. Earlier today, I asked for and was granted the hand of the lovely Miss Mary Bennet."

Mary who would never have sought to steal the spotlight from Charlotte, found - with some relief - that Charlotte was only too happy for her. For Charlotte had always thought of Mary as the Bennet sister who - like her - was most likely to suffer spinsterhood. Now, neither of them would have to live in anyone else's shadow.

In celebration of the happy news, a dinner party was planned two days hence, to include the Netherfield party (if healthy enough to travel), the Lucases and Mr. Paulson, and the Bennet household. Elizabeth was truly overjoyed at the news, for all this was *news* to her. Of course Darcy was aware and would have informed her but had yet to have an opportunity. A wistful sigh escaped her and Darcy inquired as to the cause of her discontent.

"I don't know, I guess I just miss my family. So much is happening and while I am here… I am not *here.*"

"Ah, yes. I am working on that. You see, I think it has to do with the star."

She turned to him to hide her blush from the rest of the room. "I have to admit, I was hoping our kiss would have reversed the switch."

Feigning hurt, "I hope you're not disappointed."

She smiled archly, "No, not at all. Quite the contrary. In fact, I was thinking perhaps we should try again, just in case."

"I agree."

She smiled and then, seeing her father approaching, straightened up. Mr. Bennet walked up to them and nonchalantly asked, "Mr. Darcy, do you play chess?"

"I do, Sir. Would you like to play a game?"

"Perhaps later. Rather I was wondering… have you ever been bested by a girl? I'll wager Lizzy here can give you a run for your money!"

Forgetting herself, Elizabeth smiled with obvious pride that her father would brag on her so. But Mr. Bennet took her smile for disbelief. "Come now, Lizzy, teach this young man what a real chess master looks like!" While he said it in jest, she could see Mr. Bennet was watching them both carefully. What could he mean by it?

Darcy cleared his throat, "I'd be happy to play the gentleman, *if* he thinks he's up to the challenge.

Within minutes, the three of them had set up the chess board. Elizabeth smiled at Darcy, "Ladies first."

"Thank you, *Sir*."

After an hour of intense play, they were at a stalemate. Mr. Bennet had watched fascinated as they played. It was a curious thing, Mr. Darcy had played many of Lizzy's signature moves while Lizzy had played some fairly complex moves he couldn't remember teaching her. Something was amiss but for the life of him, he couldn't figure it out. However, he had also noted that the two young people in question seemed to be two halves of a whole. It confirmed what he had been beginning to feel for some time. Lizzy, his little Lizzy, had found her match. A mixture of sadness and peace stirred within his chest. He had known this day would come; at least he could say he liked and respected this young man.

Chapter 22: Elizabeth

Elizabeth and Bingley rode into town after spending the afternoon at Longbourn. Bingley wanted to buy some small tokens for his sisters, one to help buoy Caroline's spirits and the other for Louisa and the baby - despite its arrival being months away yet. And... if he should happen to see something Jane would like, well, it wouldn't be wrong for him to buy it now and save it for when they were engaged, would it? "I plan to ask her soon, Darcy. I just don't see a reason to wait. We know each other well enough… don't you think?"

"I'm afraid I can't help you there, my friend. Only you and Miss Bennet will know when the time is right." Mr. Bingley made Elizabeth smile. He was always so amiable and genuine, and he clearly loved Jane. She would be happy to call him 'brother' soon.

As they were riding along the main street, there was a loud commotion in an alley to the side of the milliner's shop. They would have thought nothing of it but then they clearly heard someone scream.

Rushing to the scene they dismounted their horses and immediately stepped into the fray to separate the two men who were fighting. Once the scene settled, Elizabeth realized the young man whom she had helped to pull off the other gentleman was none other than Henry Wright, the stable boy from Netherfield. The gentlemen on the ground was, to no one's surprise, Wickham.

Wickham was still on the ground, bleeding so badly it was hard to recognize him at first. Only the icy blue of his eyes confirmed his identity. He was only half-conscious but he kept mumbling, saying, "It wasn't me. She's just a whore! It could have been any number of men."

"You lying bastard!" Henry lunged again and Elizabeth was barely able to hold him back. For despite Darcy's formidable size, Henry's rage gave him an advantage. Before more could be said, Wickham passed out. No one had rushed to his aide, but neither would they allow him to be further beaten.

The magistrate arrived and took control of the situation. Henry was arrested. Through tears he pleaded with Mr. Bingley to help him. "Please sir, I can explain. I know it looks bad, but I promise I can explain!"

Bingley soothed him, "Now, I am sure there is a reasonable explanation. We will see that you get a fair trial."

Elizabeth, who had known the Magistrate since she was a child, took him aside. Determined to use Darcy's wealth and status to Henry's advantage. "Mr. Hughes, that is your name, Sir, is it not?"

Mr Hughes, clearly surprised to have gained the notice of such esteemed persons as Mr. Darcy and Mr. Bingley, simply nodded.

"I have known Mr. Wickham for many years and cannot help but believe this may not be as clear cut a case as it appears. Just yesterday, I heard rumors of womanizing and gambling losses. But I think what concerns me the most is the fact that Mr. Wickham is not in uniform. Why is he out drinking in the middle of the day? I am sure you can see how all this would give me pause?"

Hanging on every word, Mr. Hughes looked very seriously at Darcy. "Yes, yes. Thank you for bringing all this to my attention. I will have to contact his superiors immediately and look into this matter."

"No need, I have already heard of the scuffle and have come to take Wickham into custody myself. If that sits well with you." Col. Forster walked up with a degree of authority that brooked no opposition. Two soldiers picked up Wickham's broken and bloodied body and dragged him to the cart waiting just outside the alley.

"Seems in addition to Lt. Wickham's womanizing - of which I was unaware until recently - he has also accrued many debts. Some so large, I am not sure he will be able to repay them. However, by far the most serious charge laid at his feet is 'Desertion'. As we are at war, he is likely facing the death penalty. Good day, gentlemen." With that the Colonel turned and walked away.

The magistrate looked at both Darcy and Bingley who wore shocked expressions. "Well, I guess that takes the charges down to Fighting in Public for Henry. If convicted, he will likely only have to pay a fine." He smiled and he tipped his hat, clearly happy not to have to follow through with a lengthy investigation. As he made his way toward the Jailhouse, he turned and added, "I'll likely be needing statements from you gentlemen later. Let me know before you go out of town so I can make sure I cross all the Ts and so on."

Straightening her clothes and making sure the crowd had dissipated, Elizabeth looked at Bingley. "You know they must have been fighting over Wickham's responsibility to Jeana?"

"Yes, I know." Bingley shook his head. "But I won't fire him," he said almost defensively. "He's a good hand and I can't say I wouldn't have done the same thing if I were in his shoes."

"Fire him? Of course not. I was thinking I would like to pay his fine. After all, he finally did what I could never bring myself to do… beat the tar out Wickham." They both chuckled as they walked back to their horses.

****

Darcy

It was not an hour after "The Brawl" - as it was being called - that word had made its way to Longbourn via Aunt Phillips. "Ladies! I have such news for you! Oh, it doesn't get any juicier than this!" Mrs. Phillips began her much anticipated gossip.

As all gathered around, Jane and Darcy listened politely but without much interest until they heard: "Mr. Bingley and Mr. Darcy".

"Well it seems that that no good, Mr. Wickham attacked young Henry Wright for no reason! Some people say it was because Henry caught him cheating at cards but I don't know. Henry doesn't strike me as a card player…"

"Aunt! What happened?" Lydia interrupted, not caring a wit whether or not she thought Henry was a card player.

"Oh well, so there he was, Wickham, beating poor Henry to a pulp, when quite out of nowhere, Mr. Bingley and Mr. Darcy rode in on their stallions. Then both leapt from down into the fray! They saved poor Henry's life! Really, he might have died if not for their bravery. Henry was arrested but isn't likely to get in any real trouble but Wickham…. Oh! His commander came and they took him away for gambling, fraternization, and DESERTION!"

Everyone gasped at mention of such a serious crime. Mrs. Phillip's continued, "I heard Col. Forster himself say Wickham would likely face the firing squad. Serves him right!"

Darcy excused himself saying, "I'm just a bit chilly. I'll just go get a shawl from my room and return shortly." Once he was up the stairs, in the safety of Elizabeth's room, he sat on the bed and wept. After all these years, it was finally over. He was free of Wickham and his insane need for revenge. Revenge for what? Darcy could only assume revenge for being born poor. The weight of so many years of disappointed hopes, worry for his loved ones, and feeling obligated to 'help' Wickham be a better man lifted from his shoulders. He sat another moment to revel in this newfound freedom, then collecting himself, he grabbed the shawl he had ostensibly come for, and returned to the parlor below.

Chapter 23: Darcy

The next day saw Darcy and the Bennet sisters returning to the modiste's for a final fitting. The ladies' dresses all fit perfectly and so were packaged to be delivered later that afternoon. Darcy was particularly pleased with Elizabeth's dress. It was flattering with a low-cut but not indecent square neckline that accentuated her figure without drawing undue attention. The cream color was complemented by the scrolling floral design in dark green with coquelicot flowers that lined the outer skirt and the center panel. The sleeves extended just past the elbow with a double layer of ruffles. As a subtle reminder, Darcy had requested pockets to be added. He smiled to himself, picturing how beautiful Elizabeth would be in this dress.

While waiting for Mrs. Bennet to finalize her transactions, he strolled through store, looking at various ribbons and baubles. Seeing a rather ornate, pearl encrusted comb, Darcy knew it cost far more than Elizabeth would ever spend on herself. However, having seen the comb, he also knew it had been made for her. He asked for it to be gift wrapped quickly, wanting to stow it away in his reticule without Mrs. Bennet or the others noticing. This comb would be his first gift, among many, that he would give to Elizabeth. He would pay her back and more, once he was back to himself.

****

Elizabeth

Elizabeth spent most of the day in Darcy's room. She had snuck some of Caroline's thread and needles that had been left in the parlor and was using them to embroider handkerchiefs for Mr. Darcy. She wanted to give him something he could not buy for himself and she knew there was little a man like Mr. Darcy wanted for. So, she sat for hours yesterday and today to add the initials "F. D." surrounded by some simple, fairly masculine scroll work in deep crimson.

Looking at her completed work, she reclined back into his luxurious bed. "Ah, I could get used to this." Before she realized it, she was fast asleep. Her dream was little more than a replay of her morning at Oakham Mount with Darcy. However, this time they were back in their own bodies and they didn't stop at a kiss. They took their time exploring each other's bodies. While she was familiar with his by now, it was very different touching Fitzwilliam, himself, with the intent to *please*. For his part, he seemed to be equally in awe. He was so gentle and yet, so passionate.

When she awoke out of breath, she was vastly relieved to be alone at Netherfield where she was unlikely to be disturbed. She took a few minutes to collect herself, studiously avoiding any direct contact with *that* area of his body. It was not that she didn't want to explore his body, she did - very much. She wanted to discover how every muscle reacted to her touch. She just wanted him to be a part of that exploration. Somehow, it would be less meaningful, almost cheap, to do so without him. When they finally came together, she wanted it to be perfect - for them both.

Elizabeth decided that she needed some distraction. She left his room and went to find Bingley. Finding him in the billiard room, she picked up a cue and prepared to re-rack the table. "Charles. What is the word on Caroline? Is she recovering well?"

"She is, she is! Much to my relief. She will likely be confined to a chair for a while yet, as she tires easily still. The doctor said she may well have permanent damage to her lungs. This morning when I checked on her she said she thought she would join us for dinner tonight." Pausing to take his shot, he then added, "I think she must be tired of her room as much as anything else."

Watching Bingley run the table, she marveled at how confident he seemed. He was not always so sure of himself. It was nice to see this side of him. Jane had been good for him. She returned to the present conversation, "Very good. And have you heard from your Aunt Matilda?"

"I have. She would love to host Caroline for the winter or longer if needed. She was also very amenable to Caroline bringing her own nursemaid. I explained that Jeana had an unusual situation. That her husband had recently been called to war and was killed soon after arriving on the continent and that we chose to keep her in our employ so she would be able to support the babe. Truth be told, I think the old bat is more excited to host the baby than she is Caroline!"

"I don't doubt it. How did Caroline take the news?"

"Er, well… I plan to tell her tomorrow night before we go to the Bennet's dinner party. She isn't well enough to join us and I figured that way she could only rant and rave for so long before we would have to take our leave. Am I a coward?" he asked, a little afraid his friend would answer honestly that he was.

"Not at all. Why should you let her berate you in your own home? She may be upset, but she will get over it. She brought this on herself. My only concern is, do you think she will agree to keep Jeana's secret?"

"I am not sure she will even know it is not true. She doesn't usually take an interest in the lives of her servants. However, I plan to threaten her that if she does not accept Jeana, she will have no maid or nurse, or even a companion at Aunt Matilda's. She will not argue, even if she doesn't like the idea."

Dinner that night was a subdued affair. Miss Bingley had entered the room on the arm of her brother, leaning heavily on his support. Elizabeth was shocked by the change in Miss Bingley. Not only did she look physically frail, but her demeanor had altered greatly as well. She seemed almost… shy or humbled.

She took her seat at the table, next to Darcy, and to Elizabeth's further surprise, she hardly spoke a word. Elizabeth tried to balance the desire to be cordial with the stronger desire not to encourage a reappearance of her earlier attentions toward the gentleman. Louisa who was glad to have her sister's company again - she had not been allowed in the sick room due to her condition - ended up monopolizing much of Miss Bingley's conversation.

Foregoing the separation of the sexes, they all gathered in the parlor after the meal. Bingley escorted his sister to a chair by the fire and placed a blanket over her lap. After a scant 30 minutes, Caroline yawned and expressed her wish to retire for the evening. Louisa, being early in her pregnancy, added her own wish to retire and implored Mr. Hurst to help them both to their rooms. However, Elizabeth caught a look that passed between the expectant parents and thought they likely had other plans for the evening that did not include sleep. *Someday,* she thought to herself, that *will be me.*

****

Darcy

That night, after dinner at Longbourn, Mr. Bennet asked Lizzy to join him in his study. Seeing the confused look on his daughter's face, he attempted to soothe her fears. "Don't worry Lizzy. You are not in trouble. But I do have some questions I want to ask of you."

Swallowing hard and hoping not to betray his extreme discomfort, Darcy simply replied, "Of course, Papa."

Once in his study, Mr. Bennet did not beat around the bush. "You and Mr. Darcy appear to have grown closer." It was not a question. "I have to say I like the young man, but I had been under the impression you did not... Clearly something has changed." He chewed on the end of his pipe, apparently thinking over his next words. "It seems to me this change came about around the same time as the Netherfield ball." Also, not a question. Darcy sat nervously, silently waiting for Mr. Bennet continue.

Smiling, Mr. Bennet went on, "I see you're not going to take pity on your poor, old Papa. What I want to know is, has Mr. Darcy made his intentions known to you?"

Despite himself, a broad smile spread across Darcy's face. "Oh well… in a manner of speaking, yes. He has told me that he loves me."

"He has told you that he loves you? But he has not asked for your hand? I am not sure how I feel about that, Lizzy." Mr. Bennet sat in his chair, a mixture of emotions swirling through him. He had known whilst watching them play chess that she was no longer his little girl. She had given her heart away.

"And you… return his feelings?"

Standing because he couldn't remain seated while expressing his feelings, "Yes, Papa. I do. You're right, something did change that night. I am not sure I can even explain it. But…"

"That's quite alright, dear. I too was once a young fool in love. However, I will expect your Mr. Darcy to apply to me for a private audience, sooner rather than later."

"Yes, Sir. I think he is just waiting for the 'right time' to do so."

Nodding, Mr. Bennet narrowed his eyes at his daughter. "That is all well and good but he best not wait too long or I may begin to think his intentions are not honorable." Then he opened his arms to his favorite daughter and beckoned her to come. Darcy hesitated only a moment and then stepped into Mr. Bennet's open arms. Whilst he never would have thought to have done so as himself, Darcy silently conceded that Mr. Bennet's loving embrace of his daughter was comforting. He had often missed his parents' affection, freely given (at least until his mother had passed away). After a few moments, Mr. Bennet released him saying, "Off you go dear. Leave your sentimental ol' papa to the comfort of his books."

Darcy left the room, filled to overflowing with hope and joy. If Mr. Bennet approved, there would be no obstacles… save one. *I wish to ask for Elizabeth's hand the right way… as myself. I don't want her to feel in any way obligated because we seem stuck with each other. I want her to know she has a choice.*

Chapter 24: Darcy

The next day was the dinner party to celebrate Mary's and Charlotte's engagements. However, Mrs. Bennet's focus was on Mary alone, much to the young lady's chagrin. But Mrs. Bennet's pride would not let her be anything less than a thorough hostess and so, every possible detail was seen to to celebrate both ladies. The meal would be decadent with three full courses, each encompassing a variety of choices from which her guests could choose.

Darcy noticed that while Mrs. Bennet spent the day giving orders for this and that to be done - doing so loudly and often repeatedly - that all was prepared well in advance of the guests arrival, leaving plenty of time to fret over what the girls would all wear. The older girls, of course, were to wear their new dresses (there would be eligible gentlemen present after all) and the youngest had been given leave to retrim their best dresses with new ribbons for the occasion. The result of so much preparation was not as Darcy expected - an overly ostentatious affair - rather it was a delightful evening with everyone looking and feeling quite marvelous.

At the appointed hour, the guests began to arrive. The Lucases were first bringing Mr. Paulson with them. He was a tall man, very thin and quiet but with a decided air of intelligence about him. Though he didn't speak often, what he did say was astute and even, on occasion clever. Darcy concluded that he would be a very good complement to Charlotte.

Some ten minutes later, Darcy began to shift his weight back and forth, impatiently looking at the parlor doors while waiting for the Netherfield party to arrive. When they finally did, Darcy noted that both Charles and Elizabeth looked a bit out of sorts. Introductions were made and Elizabeth soon joined with the group of three while Charles found Jane. And though he wanted to pull her aside to ask if everything was alright, she soon allayed his fears. "I apologize for our tardiness. Miss Bingley had thought to join us but at the last minute, was just too tired. She has not yet recovered from her recent illness." Elizabeth gave Darcy a meaningful look indicating there was more to tell but at a later time.

Dinner was served, all were suitably impressed, and toasts were made to the happy couples. Lady Lucas turned to Mary and Mr. Collins and asked, "Have you set a date yet? Charlotte has planned a spring wedding, haven't you my dear?"

Caught off guard in being addressed, Charlotte almost choked on her bite of mutton but after a quick sip of wine she recovered enough to nod. "Yes, we had thought to marry just before Easter."

Lady Lucas turned back to Mary, "And you, dear?"

Mr. Collins interrupted, "We are to wed within the month so that my bride can join me in service to our parishioners as quickly as possible."

"I still say a wedding should not be planned in such haste, but no one seems to think *my* opinions are important. I am just your mother..." Mrs. Bennet lamented.

"Mother, we talked about this. If I am to be a clergyman's wife, I need to be of service to both God and man. It is more important that I am there to serve those in need than it is for me to have a large wedding. Besides, the money wasted on these extravagant affairs really is quite ridiculous." Then seeming to realize the unintended insult that others may have perceived, she turned to Charlotte, "I don't mean to say your wedding will be a waste. I am sure it will be beautiful and... I'm sorry. You know I am just not one for the attention."

Charlotte - ever gracious - just smiled. "I know, Mary. I am not the least bit offended. In fact, I don't want a large wedding myself but Mr. Paulson is quite the social butterfly so it seems I cannot escape it!" At this Mr. Paulson protested and the room dissolved into laughter.

While everyone else was distracted with that end of the table, Darcy took the opportunity to find and squeeze Elizabeth's hand under the table. Leaning over just enough to ensure only she would hear him, he said, "I need to speak with you later." She gave a small nod and they rejoined the rest of the table's merriment.

After the meal they chose not to separate and, instead, adjourned to the parlor. Slowly but surely, larger groups broke into smaller groups and eventually the couples were able to find their way to the more isolated corners of the room. Mr. Bennet and Sir William Lucas went to his study to get away and play chess. Lady Lucas and Mrs. Bennet sat drinking tea and gossiping happily, oblivious to the rest of the room. The three youngest escaped to Lydia's bedroom probably to talk about soldiers. And Mary went to the pianoforte with Mr. Collins promising to faithfully turn pages for her.

Elizabeth looked at Darcy. They both had much to say but not in the presence of others. Looking around and seeing that everyone was engrossed in their own conversations, she whispered, "Follow my lead."

Standing, she walked over to the terrace doors and opened them. "It's a bit warm in here. Do you mind if I open the doors?" She said this to no one in particular.

Catching on Darcy followed, "Of course." No one seemed to hear or notice them. They spoke for a few more minutes before quietly inching their way out onto the terrace but the doors remained open for propriety's sake. The air was crisp but not bitter. A thousand stars could be seen and the moon was full and high.

Not wasting any time - because who knew how long they had - Darcy began. "I wanted to wait. I wanted you to choose based solely on your feelings, but it seems I cannot. I must ask you: Elizabeth, you hold my heart. You *are* my future. Even before fate intervened, I knew I could love no other." Taking her hand in his, "Elizabeth Francis Bennet, will you do me the honor of becoming my wife?"

She laughed through the tears of joy that began to fall, "Yes!" She wiped her eyes and couldn't help but tease, "but only if you promise never call me 'Francis' again."

Laughing, he quickly drew her into his embrace and kissed her passionately. It was perfect, magical even. When they pulled apart, both were filled with awe as they looked above them at the shower of stars streaking across the sky. It looked almost like fireworks there were so many. He chuckled softly, "It appears the heavens approve."

At the sound of his deep, baritone voice, Elizabeth started. "Fitzwilliam, we have switched back!" Looking down into *her* eyes, he marveled at the depth of feeling he saw in them. Pulling her to him, he reveled in the feel of having *her* in *his* arms. Placing both hands on her cheeks, he lowered his lips to hers. This time when he kissed her it was a longer, more passionate kiss. The kiss he had been yearning for for so long.

"Ahem!"

Startled, they jumped apart and turned to see Mr. Bennet standing in the doorway. "I certainly hope you are planning to come to my study in a moment, young man."

Groaning inwardly that he would have to sit through a second interview, he looked Mr. Bennet in the eyes. "Yes, Sir. I certainly am."

Turning to go back inside, Mr. Bennet said over his shoulder, "I'll expect you shortly, then." While he was not loud or demonstrative, Darcy knew Mr. Bennet meant to see his Lizzy was treated with respect.

In their remaining moments, Darcy looked at Elizabeth. "My love, you are so beautiful." He placed a soft kiss on the back of her hand. "You've made me the happiest of men, Elizabeth. And I promise, for the rest of my life, I will strive to ensure that you have all you need to make you happy."

Turning his hand over in hers, she lifted it to her lips, and not breaking eye contact, she said, "I have all I need, Fitzwilliam, as long as I have you. Now let us go inside before we garner any more attention."

As they reluctantly returned to the parlor, they received more than a few looks. But as both looked so happy, no one could wonder at what had occurred, especially when Mr. Darcy excused himself to the study. As soon as the doors shut, Jane and Charlotte gathered 'round Lizzy.

Charlotte spoke first, "So, Lizzy? Are we to wish you joy?"

Jane, uncharacteristically excited, joined in, "Oh, I do hope so!"

Lizzy blushed and smiled, 'I am so happy! Mr. Darcy has asked me to marry him… and I said 'yes'!"

The three ladies giggled and talked together and Lizzy shared how her feelings had changed. Needless to say she did not go into detail about the events of the past few weeks. If she had, they'd have thought she'd gone mad. Instead she simply reveled in the joy which abounded. Not only was she returned to herself, but she was to marry the only man she had ever loved. Elizabeth felt no other woman could be as truly blessed as she was in this moment.

Chapter 25: Darcy

"Mr. Darcy, please sit down." Mr. Bennet indicated the seat across from him. "It seems we have much to talk about."

Darcy sat and waited for Mr. Bennet to elaborate. After a moment, when it became clear that would not happen, he began, "Mr. Bennet, sir, I love Miss Elizabeth with my whole heart! I should like to have come to you sooner but, please believe me when I say, I could not. It is only tonight that I was able to ask Miss Elizabeth to marry me and since she said, "yes", now I am coming to you, sir."

"Hmm. Well, you appear to have much in your favor. You certainly are a man of means and, after making inquiries of my own, it seems you are a man of good character as well. However, it cannot surprise you that I object to my Lizzy being treated with a lack of respect. She may not be a lady of the first circles but she is a gentlewoman and she will be treated as such!"

Flustered but determined to see this through, Darcy conceded. "Yes, sir. I meant no disrespect, although I can certainly see how as her father you may feel otherwise. Forgive me."

Enjoying the younger man's discomfort, Mr. Bennet pressed on. "Mr. Darcy, I chose to believe that you were overcome with your feelings at being accepted by my daughter. I sincerely hope you understand I expect that until you are wed, there will be no more unchaperoned rendezvous on the terrace - or anywhere else."

"Yes, Sir. Of course, Sir!" It took a moment but Darcy soon realized that Mr. Benner had indirectly given his approval, if not his blessing, and slowly he began to relax.

"Now Mr. Darcy, let us get on to the business of marriage. This may seem rather indelicate but I am afraid I must ask how you plan to provide for my Lizzy. Though, as I said, I have heard of your wealth… I would like to know the truth of it from you."

While Darcy would never speak of his wealth with another under other circumstances, Mr. Bennet had every right to inquire now. So with the confidence that comes from hard work and success, Darcy began, "As I am sure you have heard, I am the Master of Pemberley in Derbyshire and Darcy House in London with an income of 10,000 a year. However, you may not be aware that I also inherited some property in Scotland worth another 4,000 a year." Seeing Mr. Bennet's eyes widen, he continued, "and I have made some very profitable investments. So, as you can see, I will have no trouble providing for a family."

"I have also heard that you are the guardian of your sister. Is that correct?"

"Yes, sir. Georgiana turned sixteen this summer. I share her guardianship with my cousin Col. Fitzwilliam - as I was quite young when my parents died."

Uncomfortable, Mr. Bennet coughed and said, "Yes, I'm sorry."

"Not at all, Sir."

"And as for pin money and the like? I have heard stories of rich men whose wives must ask permission before spending so much as a farthing. I hope you are not the overbearing type!"

At this Darcy laughed outright. Seeing Mr. Bennet's confusion he said, "I am sorry, sir, but can you see Miss Elizabeth asking me *permission* for anything?"

Mr. Bennet joined in the laughter, saying, "Quite right. I am glad you know what you are getting yourself into and that you have no plans to try to change her."

"Never. Eli… Miss Elizabeth's wit and character are what I love most about her. No woman has ever challenged me on anything. I find her honesty to be quite refreshing."

Mr. Bennet laughed again, "Just see that you still do in 30 years." They spoke some more about the details of the marriage contract but soon Mr. Bennet was satisfied that his Lizzy would be well taken care of, financially and emotionally. With his mind at ease, Mr. Bennet stood up and motioned for Darcy to join him, "Come on young man, you have a young lady waiting on you to make a rather important announcement."

****

Jane and Bingley became engaged soon after. Bingley, unhappily, felt he had to wait until he had made arrangements and sent Caroline and Jeana off to live with his aunt in Scotland. Caroline had initially railed against such degradation but eventually relented when it became clear that he would not budge. Caroline hoped that by proving herself 'reformed', their Aunt Matilda would recommend she be allowed to return to London. If not, she would only have to wait one year to reach her majority. Then no one could stop her as she would be independently wealthy and for all she cared, they could all go to Hades.

However, the day of Caroline's departure came and went and Bingley was as excited and anxious as a little boy on Christmas morning. He arose with the sun, paced the whole of the house, impatiently waiting for Darcy to arise and break his fast. Darcy entered the breakfast parlor, surprised to see his dear friend has awoken before him.

"Good morning, Charles. You are up quite early this fine day. Might I enquire if there is some pressing reason?" He added with a knowing smile, "Perhaps you are preparing for a hunt, or a trip to town to buy a new horse?"

"Darcy! It is a fine day indeed, for today I intend - as I think you have well surmised - to ride over to Longborn at the earliest acceptable hour and beg Miss Bennet to make me the happiest of men and consent to be my wife!"

The men made their way to Longborn at an hour barely acceptable by any standard but as is often the case for young love, no one begrudged them the visit. Wasting no time, Bingley suggested a walk through the garden. Elizabeth's eyes met Darcy's and they both agreed a walk sounded delightful. As the party put on their outerwear in preparation for the cold, Mr. Bennet stipulated that Kitty and Lydia should go as well to act as chaperone for all. The younger girls began to protest but seeing the firmness in their father's look, chose instead to don their coats and quietly headed out with the others.

Elizabeth and Darcy saw but said nothing as Bingley and Jane hung back from the rest of the group and then disappeared into the more secluded little wilderness to the side of the home. Once alone, Charles led Jane to the little stone bench. It was cold but neither noticed as they sat, completely lost in the moment. Charles took her hand and began his somewhat incoherent but utterly enchanting declaration of his love for her. He told her how he had known the moment he laid eyes on her that she was an angel, his angel. How throughout the time they had spent together he had only come to love her more and that he could imagine no other woman in his life… to be his partner, his wife, the mother of his children. For her part, Jane cried tears of joy and finally let herself express the depth of her feelings for him. When they rejoined the group, their smiles told all and the others immediately offered their congratulations. Back inside, Mrs. Bennet ordered Hill to prepare hot chocolate for the entire household - including the servants - such was her joy.

The weeks flew by and before they knew it Mary's wedding had come and gone. It was a modest affair but the wedding breakfast had been well attended and the happy couple made their way to Kent. Mary's first letter was filled with news of her new home, Lady Catherine's 'generous condescension', descriptions of all the parishioners she had had the pleasure of receiving, as well as the ones who had welcomed her into their homes. Elizabeth was happy for her. Mr. Collins may not be a man many women would be happy with but for Mary, he was a respectable man of God who provided her a reasonable expectation of security and fulfillment.

Mr. Darcy - with permission from Mr. Bingley - invited Georgiana and Col. Fitzwilliam to stay at Netherfield for Christmas. As expected, they got along famously with Elizabeth and her sisters. On Christmas night walking back into the parlor after a sumptuous dinner at Netherfield, Darcy pulled Elizabeth aside into a small, private alcove. Once he was sure they had not been observed, he pulled a small, soft sided package wrapped in simple brown paper. "I found this in a drawer in my room. Did you leave this… for me?"

Elizabeth colored. She had almost forgotten about the handkerchiefs. Embarrassed that she had clearly been thinking of him more than she's let on; making him gifts even. She knew it had not been proper but it had been the only way to express her growing affection for this man who would soon be her husband. Darcy took her chin in his hand and lifted her face to his. With tenderness in his eyes, he reassured her, "Do not be embarrassed my love. I adore that you thought of me. May I open it?"

Hoping he would not be disappointed, she nodded. As he slowly unwrapped and opened the package, she held her breath. "I know you have all you need. I just wanted to give you something… well, to remind you of me. At the time, I was not sure how all this would turn out."

He unwrapped the handkerchiefs that she had so lovingly embroidered. He fingered the scrollwork and looked back to Elizabeth. "They are lovely. I will cherish them and carry one with me always."

He pulled her into his embrace and whispered into her ear, "But you are not the only sly one my dear, if you look in the trunk at the foot of your bed, you will find a gift from me. Its beauty reminded me of you and I knew it must be yours. I hope you like it. But if you do not…"

Putting her fingers to his mouth she cut him off, "I am sure it will be beautiful." She added coyly, "After all, you are a man of impeccable tastes."

He leaned down and met her lips. They allowed themselves a brief moment of passion. As Darcy's kisses moved to her neck and her hands roamed freely over his chest and back pulling him closer. Before things went too far he stepped back but implored Elizabeth once more, "My darling, are you sure you don't want to elope to Scotland? We can be wed by this time tomorrow."

Pushing him away gently, she admonished, "Now Fitzwilliam, you'll just have to be patient. You only have a few more weeks to wait. Besides, we will have a week to ourselves in London while Georgiana stays here with my family before we all travel to Pemberley together. I *think* we can wait that long."

Pouting, "I suppose; if we must." They straightened up but he added, "You should go on ahead of me. I need a minute to... *compose* myself."

Before she left, she smiled one of her arch smiles and said, "Just think of something unpleasant… it worked for me when I had to *compose* myself." His mouth dropped open and she walked away, laughing before he could say a word.

Chapter 26: The Wedding

Elizabeth woke early on the day of her wedding but was not nervous. Instead, she found she could hardly sit still she was so excited. Even as she dressed and her mother gave her an awful talk about what to expect from the wedding night, all she could think about was that today she would become Mrs. Fitzwilliam Darcy. Could it really be as Mama describes it? To date, I have always enjoyed Fitzwilliam's attentions and even craved more. She remembered the sensations she had felt when they had kissed before they had switched back. It made her stomach flutter to think of it. She had catalogued those feelings with the hope and goal of bringing that pleasure to Fitzwilliam when they were finally wed. She shivered at the thought: Tonight.

Mrs. Bennet had wasted no time preparing for the wedding of the century (at least by Meryton's standards). Elizabeth's dress was to be of fine white silk embroidered with gold inlaid stitching and pearls along the bodice. She sat there staring in the mirror while Sarah worked a miracle on her hair. Looking at herself, she looked at the comb Darcy had purchased for her. It was the perfect touch and she knew he would be pleased.

After he had left and she retired to her room, she could hardly wait to find his gift. She opened her trunk and it was: a small, elegant box wrapped with a silver ribbon. She opened the box and saw the comb Darcy had purchased for her, its pearls shining in the lamp light. She gasped. "This is so beautiful." She moved to the mirror and held it up to her hair. She knew then she would save it for today.

The whole affair was to be elegant and befitting the future wife of the master of Pemberley. Truth be told, that was the only part of her new life that gave her pause… would she do him credit as Mistress of Pemberley? But Elizabeth took comfort knowing that whatever happened, he would not let her falter.

Arriving at the church, Elizabeth was overwhelmed by the beauty around her. All of her friends and family had gathered to wish her well. Lining the walls of the church were bouquets of lilies and hydrangeas in whites and purples. *He must have paid a fortune to have these brought in from a London hothouse,* she marveled.

Then she saw him - resplendent in his dark green jacket, gold vest, cream pants, and black boots - standing at the end of the aisle flanked by Col. Fitzwilliam in his most formal uniform and Mr. Bingley, also in his best. Elizabeth had chosen Jane as her maid of honor, of course. But Jane had graciously agreed to share the title with Georgiana who was ecstatic at the thought of having gained so many sisters. Elizabeth's young cousins preceded her down the aisle dropping dried, white rose petals for her to walk upon. Never in her life had she imagined such grandeur. *I suppose, I will have to get used it if I am to be Mrs. Darcy.* The thought made her smile. When her eyes met his, the rest of the world simply melted away and only the two of them remained.

The rest of the day passed by in a blur. She vaguely remembered saying her vows, attending the wedding breakfast at Longbourn, even the tearful goodbyes barely registered. All she knew for sure was that right now they were alone in her room, no *their* room, at Darcy House in London.

The fire had been built high, two plates of food had been prepared and left on the table along with a chilled bottle of champagne and two champagne glasses. It was clear they would not be disturbed.

Walking slowly toward his new bride, Darcy was determined to be gentle and to make their first experience together perfect. "Mrs. Darcy? I love how that sounds. Come to me, my love."

She did as she was bid without the least bit of hesitation. He mentally sighed with relief. He didn't want her to be scared. He began slowly. He feathered kisses over her cheeks, her eyes, and then her lips. Finally able to act on his desires, he removed the pins from her hair, running his fingers through each pinned curl.

Hearing her soft moan flamed his desire, but he forced himself to move slowly. Turning her around in his arms, he began to unbutton the long line of buttons on her dress. But he never stopped kissing her neck.

"Why are there so many of these damned things?" he said pulling at his tiny beaded nemeses.

She laughed and he growled in frustration. Finally getting the last one undone, he turned Elizabeth to him as she slid the dress to the ground. He made quick work of the remaining undergarments, taking great pleasure in each additional layer removed.

However, before removing the last layer, Elizabeth stopped him. "It is not fair, sir, that I should be so completely bare and you are still nearly fully clothed. Let me help you." She removed his shirt so that he stood before her bare chested. Remembering how sensitive his body was to touch, she slowly began to unbutton his breeches. She could see his body react and, to his surprised pleasure, it emboldened her. "I have longed to touch you like this since I first saw your bare chest in the mirror." She smiled up at him.

"Ah, so you did take advantage of our situation? You minx."

Feigning offense, Elizabeth protested, "No Sir! I was merely checking to make sure you were unscathed after a particularly rough day on horseback. What would you have thought of me if I were to return your body to you worse for the wear?"

"Um hmmm." He continued his assault on her senses as he cupped her breasts and trailed kisses down to the sensitive peaks; first one, then the other. Feeling them harden, he smiled thinking, *Ahh, yes. I remember this reaction. I enjoyed the sensation immensely.* Feeling her head drop back as she pressed into him more confirmed that she too enjoyed it.

Elizabeth was bold and curious and, having already decided to trust him fully, she gave in to her desires. They had no secrets. No fears. That night, they fulfilled those dreams they had each been struggling with. Finding pleasure in each new discovery. As they lay in bed, spent and blissfully happy, Elizabeth looked at her husband. "Fitzwilliam? Do you think we would have found each other if fate had not stepped in?"

Dragging his hand through his thoroughly tousled hair he replied, "I think the fates knew we needed a push. You are quite stubborn, after all." She protested and he laughed, but it was not long before they were in each other's arms again.

Printed in Great Britain
by Amazon

42983864R00106